THE KISS OF LIFE

THE KISS OF LIFE

Robyn Seers' romance with Dr Ross St Clair had been over and dead for two years now. She had moved to the Lake District and made a new life for herself, finding satisfaction and fulfilment in her demanding, challenging job as an ambulancewoman. So she could hardly believe it when Ross suddenly appeared on the scene, working as a local GP. Coming face to face again with him was an experience she found more traumatic than anything she ever had to deal with in her daily work...

The Kiss Of Life

by

Sarah Franklin

Dales Large Print Books
Long Preston, North Yorkshire,
BD23 4ND, England.

British Library Cataloguing in Publication Data.

Franklin, Sarah
The kiss of life.

A catalogue record of this book is
available from the British Library

ISBN   1-84262-311-7 pbk

First published in Great Britain in 1986 by Mills & Boon Ltd.

Copyright © Sarah Franklin 1986

Cover illustration © Moseley by arrangement with Allied Artists

The moral right of the author has been asserted

Published in Large Print 2004 by arrangement with
Jeanne Whitmee, care of Dorian Literary Agency

Dales Large Print is an imprint of Library Magna Books Ltd.

Printed and bound in Great Britain by
T.J. (International) Ltd., Cornwall, PL28 8RW

CHAPTER ONE

'This is one for you, Robyn.' Jim's eyes were grave as they looked into his partner's.

It had been fifteen hundred hours when the emergency call came through to Ambulance Control Centre. It was the end of the shift and Robyn and Jim were waiting to sign off for the day, but as the afternoon crew had not yet signed on, the job was theirs.

Robyn had been driver for the day and she had pulled all the stops out on the way to the warehouse, blue light revolving and the two-tone siren warning other drivers of their approach as she wove her way in and out of the traffic crowding the busy main road. Jim received further details of the incident on the radio, relaying directions to Robyn as she drove.

'It's the next right turn – the Crownhaven road,' he told her. 'The large warehouse close to the docks. A young guy was doing some maintenance work when a load of girders being winched on to a lorry fell on him. It sounds bad.'

Robyn had felt the familiar surge of adrenalin as she pressed her right foot hard down to the floor of the ambulance.

But now they had arrived and Jim, taking in the situation at a glance, began to herd the anxious onlookers out of the way. The victim had been painting a gallery on one side of the warehouse when one of the chains holding a heavy load of steel girders broke, releasing its load on to the unsuspecting man and pinning him where he lay. The foreman who had made the 999 call joined them.

'There's a small space.' He pointed to the grotesque tangle of metal, his face white with shock and anxiety. 'If someone could climb up and squeeze through–' he left the sentence unfinished. 'We didn't dare risk it in case we shifted the load.' That was when Jim had nodded to Robyn and said: 'This is one for you, I'm afraid, love. You're the only one small enough to get through there.'

Without a second prompting she strapped on the hard hat he handed her and, giving Jim her emergency satchel to hold, hauled herself up on to the platform, moving gingerly so as not to disturb the scatter of girders that pinned the man down.

Squeezing through the gap, she made eye-to-eye contact with the victim, and her heart contracted as she saw that he wasn't more than seventeen years old.

'Soon have you out of here,' she said quietly. 'But we shall need your help. What's your name?'

The fair-haired boy's features were contorted with pain as he gasped: 'Daniel.'

'Right, where does it hurt, Daniel?' While she was talking, Robyn was busy, making what examination she could in the limited space. She could see that the boy's arm was twisted behind him and that there was an evil-looking open wound in his leg, which was clearly fractured, but most serious of all was the fact that most of the weight was on his stomach. 'Does your leg hurt?' she asked. 'Can you move it?'

He swallowed hard. 'No. Can't feel the legs – it's my stomach.' His teeth were chattering. Robyn took his pulse. Its rate, along with his respiration, was very high and his colour was poor, his brow clammy with sweat.

She touched his cheek. 'Right, hold on. I'll be back. Don't try to move – and don't worry. Just trust us.'

Back on the warehouse floor she spoke

urgently to Jim. 'We're going to need a medical team. Can you radio for IVES? There are multiple injuries and almost certainly internal bleeding; probably from a ruptured spleen.'

He nodded. 'We'd better have the fire brigade too – to shift that lot we'll need lifting gear, and I'll alert Crownhaven General A and E while I'm there.' Jim handed her the emergency satchel he had been holding for her, along with the Entonox gas apparatus he had fetched from the ambulance while she was with the victim. 'Will you set up a drip?'

Robyn shook her head. 'I'd like to, but I don't think I can risk that much movement until some of the weight has been lifted.' Jim nodded as she began to climb back on to the platform.

'Right, I'll get the call through at once. You'll need the portable oxygen pack too.'

Forty-year-old Jim had fifteen years experience behind him, but he had the greatest admiration for the diminutive, dark-haired girl who was his new partner. There wasn't two-pennyworth of her, he reflected; she wasn't much bigger than his own twelve-year-old daughter, yet when she went into action like this there was no one in the unit to beat her. The warehouse foreman followed him to the ambulance, anxious to help all he could.

'She's a plucky lass,' he said. 'I'll admit that when I saw her coming my heart sank – slip of a kid like that. But she seems to know what she's doing all right.'

'She does,' said Jim, his jaw set grimly. 'And she's no kid, believe me. Robyn Seers is a fully trained paramedic; the best we've got. I only wish that kind of training had been available in my day.'

After Robyn had the Entonox mask in place and the boy had taken a few deep breaths he began to relax a little, the pain easing. Robyn lay on her stomach, the mass of tangled girders suspended above her, her face close to the victim's.

'Where do you live, Danny?' she asked. 'With your parents?'

'Just Mum,' he whispered. 'Dad died two years ago.'

'Any brothers and sisters?'

'No, just us.'

'Have you got any pets?' – Anything to take his mind off the blue steel menace, hanging over them. 'Is this your first job, Danny?'

Daniel's voice was ragged as he said: 'Not

a job really – Youth Opportunities scheme.' He gave her a wry smile. 'Making a right pig's ear of it, aren't I?'

Robyn held the small black face mask in postion, feeling the shudders of tension passing through the boy's body as she did so, watching the sweat and tears mingle as they trickled down his cheeks.

'Hang on, love,' she whispered. 'Not long now. Fire brigade's on its way, then we'll soon have you out.' But after a few more minutes she could see that inhaling the Entonox gas was becoming too much of a strain. Edging backwards, she reached down for the oxygen equipment Jim had brought her. He handed it up, his face concerned as he peered up at her.

'Are you all right, love? Shall I try and take over?'

She shook her head. 'No, I'm fine.'

Daniel's colour improved a little with the oxygen and a few minutes later Robyn allowed herself a sigh of relief when she heard the emergency siren of the first brigade rescue tender as it drove up outside. The skilled men quickly assessed the situation, then began to set up their equipment. As she waited, Robyn talked to her patient – about anything and everything under the sun. She must keep him reassured and as alert as she could. Inwardly she was worried; his condition was clearly deteriorating before her eyes, and until the weight was lifted from him there was so pathetically little she could do. She knew the firemen were doing their best, yet the minutes seemed to tick by agonisingly slowly.

At last they were ready. Jim told her from below that a doctor had arrived, a member of the Integrated Voluntary Emergency Service made up of local GPs. He was ready and waiting. The men would lift the weight of girders and hold them just long enough for the removal of the patient. Could she hang on another few minutes?

'I can.' She looked at Daniel's ashen face and added under her breath: 'I only hope *he* can.'

She heard the muffled conversation going on between Jim and the newly arrived doctor, and a moment later another figure wearing a hard hat began to edge on to the platform behind her. She half turned her head, wincing at the movement he was creating.

'For God's sake be careful,' she warned between clenched teeth.

The movement stopped. 'The firemen

have a temporary grip on the relevant girders, but before they lift can you tell me what diagnosis you've been able to make?' His voice was quiet and calm, but the Scottish accent with its velvet smoothness made her catch her breath. If she hadn't known he was thousands of miles away she would have sworn... She collected her thoughts rapidly.

'There's internal bleeding,' she told him briskly. 'Probably from a ruptured spleen – open fracture of the right tibia, a fractured arm and almost certainly crushed ribs. I've done what I can, but he's barely conscious now. There's no time to lose.'

The man behind her drew an uneasy breath. 'Right. Get a grip on his shoulders, ready to help me pull him clear when they lift the mass off him. Are you ready?'

Robyn moistened dry lips. 'But if his spine is injured? It's more than likely...'

'We've no choice,' he told her abruptly. 'One slip and we could lose him altogether. I take it *you'd* quite like to go on living for a while too? I know I would!'

Robyn gripped the lad's shoulders firmly, her muscles tense as she waited for the word of command from the fireman below. Inwardly she seethed at the doctor's attitude.

She was well aware of the dangers. It wasn't the first time she had put her life on the line to help a patient; it was one of the hazards of her job and she didn't need him to warn her. If only there had been the time and space to have immobilised the boy's limbs to ensure the least possible damage to his spinal cord.

But there was no time for further thought. The fireman gave the command and Robyn held her breath as the sound of grinding metal echoed round the huge building. The tension felt by everyone watching was an almost tangible presence as the mass was lifted a few creaking inches and they heaved the semi-conscious boy out from under it. A moment later willing hands were helping to ease him gently down and on to the waiting stretcher. It was only then that Robyn and Dr Ross St Clair looked into each other's faces for the first time.

Robyn gave an audible gasp of shock, and Jim grasped her arm.

'Are you all right, Robbie?'

But the shock that had set her head reeling was nothing to do with the ordeal she had just handled so efficiently. She squared her shoulders.

'I'm fine, thanks, Jim.'

In the ambulance she prepared to set up a

drip while Ross St Clair examined the patient. As he covered the boy he looked up at Robyn.

'I think I'd better travel with him to the hospital,' he said, then quietly; 'I have to say that you were the last person I expected to find at the scene of the accident!'

She felt the hot colour suffuse her face as she looked directly into the steel blue eyes. She had recognised his voice the moment he had spoken, but she had refused to acknowledge the recognition. Hadn't it happened a thousand times before? Hadn't she congratulated herself only recently that she had stopped seeing his face in every crowd? It had seemed vaguely odd to her that she should start imagining such things in a situation of extreme urgency and she had pushed it impatiently to the back of her mind, dismissing it as all part of the tension. After all, it *couldn't* be Ross, she told herself. He was thousands of miles away, in Saudi Arabia.

But now, face to face with the tanned face and thick copper hair, the deep blue eyes that were staring so incredulously into hers, there was no denying it.

Crimson-faced, she edged past him, ignoring his remark. 'We'd better get going.

There's no time to be lost.' She stepped out of the ambulance and looked at Jim, who was watching her with a slightly puzzled expression.

'No need for you to drive after what you've just gone through,' he told her. 'You're as white as a ghost. I'll take over. You stay inside with the patient in case the doc needs help.'

But she was already climbing into the driving seat. 'I'd rather complete the day properly, if you don't mind, Jim.' She started the engine, engaging first gear and switching on the revolving blue light as she edged the vehicle out through the warehouse yard gates.

At Crownhaven General Daniel went straight to the theatre after the consultant and Dr Ross St Clair had conferred. When they had wheeled him away Robyn looked at Jim.

'Can we wait, just for a while, to see if he's going to make it?'

The older man looked into the large pleading blue eyes, then doubtfully at his watch. 'OK, though we should get the vehicle back.' He frowned at her. 'What's up? I've never seen you get as involved as this, Robbie.'

She sighed. 'If he's got spinal injuries, dragging him out like that won't have helped.'

Jim touched her arm and felt her trembling. 'Take it easy, love. You were working under the doc's supervision, after all. No one's going to blame you. You did a very courageous job.'

'What does that matter, for God's sake?' she snapped. 'It won't be any use telling *him* that if he's paralysed!' She ran a hand through her dark, curly hair and gave him an apologetic smile. 'Sorry, Jim – I guess it's the wrong end of the day for this kind of thing. I know you're right really. It's just that he's so young. He told me his mother is a widow too. I daresay he's all she's got.'

They sat in the waiting area in Accident and Emergency, sipping tea that Jim fetched from the vending machine as they waited for news. At last Jim touched her arm and her heart quickened as she looked up to see Ross coming towards them.

'He's going to be all right,' he said briefly.

Robyn looked at him. 'His back–?'

He shook his head. 'His injuries are pretty extensive – impossible to tell just how bad till some of the bruising and swelling have reduced. But the emergency op will deal with the bleeding.' He smiled. 'You were right about the spleen– Don't worry, his youth and strong constitution will pull him through.'

'His mother,' Robyn muttered. 'His mother's a widow. He told me...'

'She's on her way here. The police have informed her.' Ross looked at her hard, glancing briefly at Jim. 'I'd like to talk to you, but you look all in. Can I take you home?'

She shook her head. 'I have to go back to Control to sign off.' For the first time she looked down at herself. Her blue uniform jersey and trousers were streaked with dirt. She lifted a hand to her face and hair. She must look a mess. 'I – I'll have a shower and change there before I go home.'

'I'll be in touch,' he told her. 'I must report back to the surgery now.' She watched as he walked away, tall and broad-shouldered, his fiery head held at that proud angle she knew so well.

Jim stood up. 'Come on, love, let's get you back to Control. And this time I'm driving. You're off duty as from now – no arguments!'

Back in the ambulance the older man glanced at his partner. She looked preoccupied. He spoke hesitantly.

'I haven't come across Dr St Clair before. Seems you have, though.'

She sighed, dragging her thoughts back to the present. She felt unequal to a full-scale explanation of her relationship with Ross. It was such a long and complicated story, and anyway, it was private; painfully so.

'I met him at the hospital in London where I did my paramedic training,' she told him, trying to sound unconcerned and casual. 'At that time he was a houseman for the consultant I trained under.'

Jim nodded, his eyes on the road. Quite clearly there had been more than just a passing acquaintance between the two, but he wasn't going to push it.

'A coincidence, him turning up here. He must have recently joined one of the local group practices on the IVES register.'

Robyn nodded. 'I suppose so. The last I heard he was going abroad – he'd landed a highly paid job in Saudi Arabia.' She shrugged. 'Maybe it didn't work out.'

She sank back in her seat, too weary now to stop the memories from flooding back. Seeing them speaking so casually this afternoon how could Jim have guessed that for a whole year she and Ross St Clair had shared a life together – that Ross had been her whole world? She had truly believed that she had been his too, until everything turned sour and he had shown himself as self-seeking and ruthless.

It was almost two years since they had split up and gone their separate ways, yet coming face to face with him like that this afternoon had torn the wound open again in the most devastating way. Along with the trauma of the warehouse rescue it was almost more than she could do to hide her anguish.

At the Control Centre she signed off in the day book, showered and changed into her own clothes, then made her way to the car park.

Alone in her car she relaxed, releasing the tight control that had hidden her feelings. For a while she sat there, allowing her thoughts to drift. How many times had she dreamed of such a situation, imagining the calm with which she would cope with it, the icy coolness that would prove to Ross that she was over him?

She had come up here to the Lake District to get away from all the old associations – to make a new start. It had taken her a year to settle down and she was just beginning to enjoy the varied life spent working between

23

the small industrial town of Crownhaven and the wild, beautiful countryside beyond its boundaries. She hadn't found it easy at first to make friends. Unlike her previous job where the mix of male and female personnel was fairly even, here at Crownhaven most of her colleagues were male and married. But six months ago she had met Fay Scott, a staff nurse at the local hospital, with whom she now shared a cottage. Recently she had begun to go out with Bill Hughes, a reporter on the *Crownhaven Courier.* Bill had contacted her when she first arrived in the town, asking if he could do a piece on ambulancewomen for his paper. She smiled to herself as she remembered their first meeting.

'I thought I'd angle it from the Women's Lib viewpoint,' he'd suggested. He had been surprised when she had told him that for a long time ambulancewomen had been treated as equals as far as pay and status were concerned.

'That must mean that you have to do exactly the same jobs!' he'd said, looking slightly startled.

'Of course. That's only fair,' Robyn told him.

He'd looked sceptically at her slight build.

'You don't look strong enough – for the lifting and so on.'

She laughed. 'Well, I admit that at five foot three I only just scraped in on height. As for the rest, it's a matter of training.'

'Ah yes...' Bill's pencil hovered over his notebook. 'I'm sure our readers would be interested to hear about that. Did you have to train as a nurse first?'

Robyn had explained that her training was in fact quite different from that of a nurse because as well as the obvious theory and practical work she had had to take an advanced driving course. Being able to drive speedily and skilfully in heavy traffic was essential, as well as being able to handle any of the differing vehicles used by the ambulance service. Then there were rescue procedures to learn and a thorough working knowledge of all the emergency equipment to acquire.

'I see – great.' Bill had looked at her, his eyes twinkling wickedly as he asked the next question.

'And all that free time – lounging about between calls. How do you fill that in?'

Robyn had bristled – which was exactly what he had intended. *Free time?* she exclaimed. 'I just wish you could see the amount of paperwork we have to do! Every call has to be written up, you know. Then there's all our equipment to check and keep in good order – our vehicle to maintain. And you can't relax, you know. At any time an emergency call could come through and you have to be on your toes, ready to leap into action.'

Bill grinned. 'All sounds pretty tense! But what about the night shifts? Surely those are less busy?'

'They are often quieter,' she admitted. 'And we're allowed to watch television or play cards and so on, but that's also when you can study for promotion. That's how I got to be a paramedic. As I told you, there are as many opportunities for women as for men in the service – as long as you're prepared to work as hard.'

'I see. So being a paramedic is – what?' He looked up at her, the pencil poised again as she explained that a paramedic is allowed to work on his or her own diagnosis, to administer certain drugs and to perform emergency treatments such as intubation.

'It entails an extra period of training in a teaching hospital,' she told him. 'Working under a consultant anaesthetist – in the operating theatre and in the maternity unit and accident and emergency department.'

Bill was beginning to look at her with more than a hint of admiration in his eyes. 'This is really opening my eyes,' he told her. 'You know, I thought that two people went around in an ambulance – one to drive and one to do the ministering angel bit.'

'That was the case once. But obviously it makes for better efficiency if both are equally trained.'

Bill had rung on the day the article appeared in the paper to ask if she approved and ended by asking her out. Robyn liked his zany sense of humour and they had had some happy times together. She had really begun to pick up the pieces – to feel a whole person again. Now this had to happen.

She frowned as she remembered Ross's words at the hospital: 'I'd like to talk to you. I'll be in touch.' Why couldn't he leave it alone? It was over and dead, their affair. Surely he didn't intend to exhume it; wouldn't be so cruel as to try to disrupt her life again? To her extreme annoyance she felt an involuntary tingle of excitement deep inside at the thought and was reminded, not for the first time, of how perfidious the human heart can be.

Angrily she fished her ignition key out of

her handbag and started the car, nosing it out of the car park and on to the road, filtering into the late afternoon traffic swiftly and skilfully, glad to have something to take her mind off that poor boy back at the hospital – of Ross and the unquiet thoughts his reappearance had awakened.

As she drove she flexed her neck and shoulders, feeling the creaking tension that still gripped the muscles. It had been a hard day. It would be good to get home.

Fell Cottage was one of a small cluster of fishermen's houses that made up the village of Ravenshore, on the edge of a small inlet of the West Lancashire coast. It had a view of the sea and mountains from the front windows and the rising fells at the back. Robyn still couldn't quite believe her luck at living in such a beautiful place. The cottage belonged to a local doctor who had once used it as a holiday home. He had retired now and gone south to live. At first he had let the cottage to holidaymakers, but when Fay, who had been at school with his daughter, had asked him if she and a friend might have it on a permanent basis he had agreed readily.

It was a six-mile drive from Crownhaven, but neither of them minded that. It was well worth it to live in such a lovely place. But this evening Robyn was too preoccupied even to savour the view as she put the car away and went in by the back door of the cottage. As she took off her coat in the little lobby where originally fishermen's oilskins had hung, she sniffed. Fay was on nights and it was obvious that she had been cooking. A savoury aroma of chicken casserole drifted out, reminding Robyn that she hadn't eaten since the hurried sandwich she had snatched at lunchtime. She opened the door to see Fay standing at the cooker, her face flushed with the warmth. She smiled.

'Oh good, you're back at last. I was just beginning to wonder…' She stopped, peering closely at her friend. 'Are you all right? You look absolutely all in!'

Robyn sank on to a chair at the kitchen table. 'We had an emergency just as we were about to sign off. It was at that big ware-house near the docks. A load of steel girders fell on a young boy.'

Fay winced. 'Oh God! Was he…?'

Robyn shook her head. 'He's alive – bad, though. It was touch and go. We had to pull him clear and I'm worried about his spine. Jim and I waited at the hospital, but he was still in surgery when we left. They say he'll live, though.'

Fay opened the cupboard and poured sherry into a glass which she handed to Robyn. 'Here, drink this, you look as though you need it. It's only cooking sherry, I'm afraid, but it'll help.' She frowned as she watched her friend sip from the glass.

'I know it's upsetting, but you must have seen a dozen such cases. Why has this one got to you so badly? Did you have to take the decision to pull him free on your own? Wasn't there a doctor there?'

Robyn gave a short laugh. 'Oh yes, there was a doctor there. He made the decision; the only one possible. It isn't that so much.' She sighed, twisting the stem of her glass, as Fay turned back to the cooker.

'Well, I'd better dish this up. I hope you haven't lost your appetite.'

A few minutes later as they ate together Fay glanced again at Robyn. 'Look, do you want to talk about it? I can see something has happened – something shattering by the look of it.' When Robyn hesitated she added: 'I really do want to help, you know. It's not just morbid curiosity.'

Robyn looked up. 'I know you do. And I do want to talk to someone. It's just so difficult to know where to begin. This afternoon I had quite a shock. A piece of my past turned up again.'

Fay got up to pour the coffee. 'In what shape?'

'Human,' Robyn said briefly. 'At the warehouse Jim radioed for a medical team – you know, the Integrated Voluntary Service. The doctor who arrived was new in the district…'

'But not new to you?' Fay suggested.

Robyn nodded unhappily. 'I met Ross when I was training in London, and we fell in love. At least *I* did. He said he didn't want to marry until he'd built his career. He had great ambitions to be a consultant before he was forty. I was so besotted that I told myself it was a good idea. I wanted to build my own career anyway, so I persuaded myself that he was right and it would be better not to be tied down. We found a flat and moved in together instead.'

Fay waited, watching Robyn stir her coffee for a while before she said gently: 'You've hinted before that there was someone special in your life. So what went wrong?'

'Nothing at first. In fact I was happier during that year than I can ever remember being, before or since. Then Ross applied

31

for a job in Saudi Arabia. It offered fantastic money, you see.' She looked up quickly. 'Ross wanted to save so that he could take a year off to study under a Swiss surgeon who was doing some remarkable work in the transplant field.' Aware that she sounded defensive, she coloured slightly and lifted her cup to take a sip.

Fay nodded. 'So he went away and left you flat. Is that it?'

Robyn smiled wistfully. 'It wasn't quite as simple as that. Sometimes I think I could have coped with that situation better.' She sighed as she put her cup down, painful memories flooding back. 'I was prepared for us to part. We'd always agreed that if either of us got a good opportunity we'd put it first,' she explained. 'So when Ross told me he'd got this job I was quite prepared for our relationship to end. Then, out of the blue, he asked me to marry him and go too.' She shook her head. 'I reacted like a complete fool. I forgot all the promises we'd made. I was ready to throw everything up and follow him. Then I found out *why* he'd asked me!'

Fay frowned. 'What do you mean – why he'd asked?'

'For that kind of job – in a place like Saudi Arabia a wife is a fairly necessary part of the qualifications. It isn't an easy place to live in, apparently. The pressures are pretty tough at times and it was felt that a married man was preferable. All this came out bit by bit. Gradually I got the picture. Ross wanted that job very badly – so he'd assured them that he would be a married man by the time the appointment was confirmed! As simple as that. No thought for me or my career. He'd even anticipated my response.'

'So what happened?' asked Fay.

Robyn shrugged. 'We had a row.' She smiled wryly. 'That sounds like the under-statement of all time. We had the *mother and father* of all rows, and I left. I felt used and humiliated. If I'd ever wondered if Ross really loved me I knew the answer. He didn't. I was just a handy person to have around, and when the need for a wife cropped up – well, I was as good as anyone, I suppose. And to think I almost gave up my career for that! I asked him point blank if he would have given up everything for me, and he agreed that he wouldn't, but he seemed to think *that* was different!' Robyn folded her arms on the table and sighed. 'It was almost two years ago that I walked out of the flat we shared. I heard later that he'd gone to Saudi Arabia after all, but apart from that I haven't seen or heard of him again until this afternoon. So you can guess what a shock it was.'

'He never tried to get in touch then – to find out where you were?' Fay asked.

Robyn shook her head. 'I said some pretty hard things to him, so it wasn't exactly surprising. I feel a bit ashamed when I look back – but I was badly hurt. You see, Ross knew how much my career meant to me, but he took advantage of the fact that I loved him enough to give it up. That's what I couldn't forgive.'

'I can understand that. And now?' Fay reached out to touch her arm.

Robyn sighed. 'I really thought I was over him. I'd started to be happy again. Lately I've been thinking how well everything has turned out for me. The job, you, and more recently, Bill.' She looked up, tears starting to fill her eyes. 'Oh, Fay … I'll have to move, to leave here. I couldn't go through all that again. I just *couldn't!*'

Fay patted her shoulder. 'I'm sure it won't come to that, love. There could be an explanation. Maybe he's only here temporarily, as a locum for one of the doctors. Why don't you just sit tight and see what happens?' She looked at her watch, beginning to get up

34

from the table. 'I'm going to have to run now. Have a good night's sleep. Things always look better in the morning.'

'Yes, you're right, of course.' Robyn got up and began to clear the table. 'You go and get ready to go on duty. I'll clear up. It'll help to have something to do.'

The cottage was quiet when Fay had gone, so quiet that Robyn wondered how she would stand it. Usually she loved the serene peace of the little village after a busy day, but tonight she would have given anything to have been on duty; to have thrown herself into the bustle of the busy ambulance base.

She was just wondering whether to go for a walk along the shore when there was a knock on the door and she opened it to find Bill standing on the doorstep, a big smile on his face and a bunch of flowers in his hand. She stared in surprise at the expressive face topped by a thatch of tousled fair hair and said abruptly:

'What are you doing here?'

His face dropped in comic dismay. 'Well, that's a nice welcome, I must say!' He pushed her gently inside and closed the door. 'I had a sudden telepathic message that you were alone and fed up,' he told her. 'So here I am. The Bill Hughes de luxe cheering up service is at your disposal for the evening – on the house.'

Robyn eyed him suspiciously. 'That telepathic message wasn't passed to you over the telephone by a willowy blonde whose initials are F.S, was it?'

Bill's mobile face assumed its innocent look. 'It's the thought that counts, isn't it?'

She frowned. 'I wish she hadn't done that. What did she say?'

He shrugged. 'Not a lot. Just that you'd had a hell of a day and needed cheering up.' He smiled wistfully at her, unwinding the striped college scarf he always wore. 'You know I don't need much of an excuse, don't you?'

Robyn relaxed, looked at the flowers. 'Are those for me?' She took them from him. 'I'd better put them in water.'

She found a vase and began to arrange the flowers. Bill threw the scarf over the back of a chair and came up to slip his arms around her waist.

'What was it that upset you today, Robbie?' he asked, his lips close to her cheek. 'Was it just the pressure of work, or did something happen?'

Briefly she wondered if Fay had said more than he'd admitted, then he added:

'There's nothing I wouldn't do for you, Robbie. I think you know that by now, don't you?'

She turned in the circle of his arms, looking up into his eyes. They were brown, twinkling eyes, but at this moment they were uncomfortably serious, and she knew a sudden pang. She didn't want to fall in love again. She didn't want anyone to fall in love with her either. It was all too heavy. Her friendship with Bill had been such fun – so far. She kissed him lightly on the cheek.

'Of course. And there's nothing I wouldn't do for you either, so let's keep it like that, eh? – doing nothing for each other.'

But he wasn't to be put off by her flippancy. He pulled her close, his lips coming down on hers in a slightly tremulous kiss that told her how deeply his feelings went. And although she had told herself she wasn't ready for another relationship she couldn't help responding to its warmth and sensitivity. Bill was so nice, so safe. Here in his arms like this she could forget everything else. As the kiss ended she buried her head against his shoulder and sighed.

'I need time, Bill,' she murmured. 'I've told you that, haven't I?'

'I know,' he whispered against her hair.

'And you can have it. Just as much as you need. I know when I'm on to a good thing, and if it's a question of simply waiting...'

The telephone shattered the intimate atmosphere, making them both start. Robyn looked at him. 'How about putting the kettle on for some coffee while I answer that?'

In the hall she snatched up the receiver. 'Hello, Ravenshore 218.'

'Robyn, it's Ross. When can we meet?'

She stifled a gasp. It was so typical. *'When* can we meet?' Not, *'Can* we?' 'I wasn't aware that we'd arranged to meet,' she said icily.

She heard him sigh at the other end of the line. With great patience, as though she were a wayward child having a tantrum, he went on:

'It's obvious we're going to have to meet and talk. You know that as well as I do. If we're to be working in the same area it's inevitable that we'll run into each other from time to time. It could – well, make life unnecessarily complicated.'

Her heart sank. 'I see. You're here permanently, then?'

'But of course. What did you imagine?'

'That you were filling in; doing locum work–' she trailed off weakly.

There was a pause before he said tartly: 'Sorry to disappoint you, but I'm here for good.'

'I could always move,' she said. 'Maybe that would be best.'

'Why on earth should you do that?' His voice was impatient. She remembered the tone so well, and anger began to quicken her heartbeat.

'Look, Robyn, we're responsible adults, not children,' Ross reminded her. 'What happened between us was over a long time ago. I see no reason why it should go on disrupting our lives. Neither do I see any reason why we shouldn't meet and talk it through like sensible people. Are you free tomorrow?'

She felt as though the breath had been dashed from her body. 'Yes,' she managed to whisper.

'Right. It's my day off. I'll meet you by the park gates in Crownhaven at eleven o'clock – all right?'

'I suppose so, if you insist, though I really can't see...' Robyn stopped speaking, staring at the buzzing receiver in her hand. He had rung off, exploding her peace of mind, shattering her anticipation of a tranquil evening with Bill; ruining her hopes of a new and uneventful life.

She stood in the hall, staring at the silent telephone. 'I hate you, Ross St Clair,' she said aloud. 'When I see you tomorrow I'll *tell* you so. It will give me the greatest pleasure!'

CHAPTER TWO

It was exactly eleven o'clock when Robyn arrived at the gates of Crownhaven Municipal Park. She looked around; Ross wasn't there. He never could keep an appointment on time, and she felt a stab of annoyance, imagining the eyes of passers-by staring at her as she waited by the ornate wrought iron gates. The entrance to the park was an avenue of beautiful mature maples, now turning a glorious golden russet. She decided to go for a walk. If he arrived then let *him* hang around and wait for her.

She walked the length of the avenue, watched the ducks on the ornamental lake for a while, then walked back towards the gates. As she came in sight of them again she saw him. He seemed relaxed and unconcerned as he glanced each way, and she toyed with the idea of turning back and making him wait longer, but after a moment's hesitation she abandoned the idea. She wasn't looking forward to the coming discussion. The sooner they got it over and done with, the better.

Drawing nearer, she saw that Ross wore a grey suit. Grey had always suited him, complementing his russet colouring perfectly.

He turned as she drew level with him and his eyes flicked over her, taking in the red coat, the dark curls framing the small piquant face, rosy with colour from her brisk walk in the crisp autumn air. He looked pointedly at his watch.

'I thought I said eleven o'clock.'

'You did,' she said. '*I* was here. Where were you?'

He looked again at his watch. 'I have an appointment at twelve. No time to argue about who was on time and who wasn't. Shall we go somewhere for coffee?'

'As you like.' Inwardly she seethed. He hadn't forgotten how to divert attention when he was in the wrong!

He took her arm and hurried her towards the Grand Hotel on the opposite side of the road, walking so fast that she had almost to run to keep up. In the lounge, discreetly seated at a table behind a potted palm, Ross ordered coffee from an elderly waiter, then looked at her, his face breaking into a sudden smile.

'This place is straight out of Oscar Wilde,

42

isn't it? You expect Lady Windermere to step out from behind the palms at any minute!'

Robyn caught her breath, completely taken aback. How could she have forgotten the disarming sweetness of that smile and the effect it had always had on her? The steel blue eyes seemed to soften to the colour of a summer sky, crinkling attractively at the corners, the cleft in his chin deepened, and the mouth... She stared helplessly at the sensuously curved lips, remembering with alarming clarity how it felt to be kissed by them. Shock spread the warm colour from her neck to her hairline and her gloved hands clenched in her lap. He leaned forward to cover one of them with his own.

'Robyn, I hope you believe me when I say that it's good to see you. I admit that it was a bit of a shock, running into you like that yesterday, but nevertheless...'

As she heard his voice, speaking softly and intimately – sitting here close to him like this, her mind drifted. She was remembering so much about him; such silly little things. Did he still have a passion for avocados? Had he conquered that irritating habit of leaving the top off the toothpaste tube? Sitting here drinking coffee it was as though the past two years were as many hours. Ross had always known how to disarm – how to get his own way. Clearly he hadn't lost the skill. She mustn't let herself be sweet-talked all over again.

Steeling herself to meet his gaze, she looked up, hoping her voice was achieving just the right note of nonchalance as she said:

'It's good to see you too, Ross, now that the initial shock is over. Tell me how you come to be here in Crownhaven.'

Before he could speak again the coffee arrived. He thanked the waiter and looked at her, raising an eyebrow.

'Are you going to do the honours?'

She poured the coffee, wondering whether he knew how mocking his words sounded. Avoiding his eyes, she passed him his cup.

'As you'll have guessed, I'm with one of the local group practices,' he told her casually. 'With Dr Muir and his partners.'

Robyn's head was spinning. There were so many questions milling round inside it. Ross had always been so ambitious. During their time together he had been adamant in his decision not to follow in his father's footsteps. Dr Greg St Clair had practised medicine in the small Highland town where he was born for the whole of his working

44

life. Ross had wanted so much more, had intended to carve out a place for himself, to be among the top men in his field. He had studied hard for his fellowship, intending eventually to research into cardiac surgery. That had been his reason for wanting to remain free. Why then had he settled for a place in a group practice in the Lake District?

She lifted her cup and took a sip. 'Yes, naturally I guessed that.' She longed to ask some of the questions that tumbled through her mind, but steeled herself not to.

'Saudi Arabia didn't work out as I'd expected,' he said. 'I felt I was wasting time, so I came home to England, saw this opportunity and took it.'

'I would have expected you to have taken something more – well, high-powered,' she ventured. 'General practice was never one of your career priorities, as I remember.'

His mouth hardened. 'People change, you know.'

'I do know. It's just that I'd have thought...' She broke off as she saw a flicker of annoyance darken his eyes. 'I'm sorry, it's none of my business, of course.' There was an awkward pause. Robyn took another sip of her coffee then looked at him tentatively.

45

'Obviously you didn't come here to discuss your career with me. What was it you wanted to talk about?'

'I think you know perfectly well what we have to talk about.' The impatience was still there in his eyes. It stung her into saying:

'If you're afraid I'm going to embarrass you in some way, Ross, you can forget it. We knew each other a long time ago. Now we find ourselves working in the same town again. It's not world-shattering. I see no reason why the situation should inconvenience either of us in any way.'

The coolness of her voice belied the thudding of her heart. Inwardly she was astonished at the words she heard coming out of her mouth. Only last night she had spoken in that panic-stricken way to Fay about leaving Crownhaven. Now here she was talking as though Ross's presence mattered nothing to her.

She looked up at him. Was that relief she read in his eyes? She should have been glad that her acting was so convincing, but, perversely, her heart sank. Clearly he was anxious to shake the dust of the past off once and for all.

'I'm glad you see it that way,' he said stiffly. 'Obviously after all this time we've both made a new life. Things have changed quite dramatically for me and I daresay they have for you too. It would be stupid to let the past disrupt things.' He looked at her and added quickly: 'For either of us.'

Robyn tried to smile convincingly, but the corners of her mouth dragged downwards. 'Of course. After all, what happened between us was over a very long time ago,' she said lightly. 'I daresay we've both formed new relationships by now.' She glanced at him, but his expression told her nothing. 'I have,' she added.

Ross drained his cup and passed it to her to refill. Sitting back in his chair, he look relaxed as he crossed one immaculately grey-trousered leg over the other.

'Good!' he said smilingly. 'Now, tell me all about your career and what you've been doing since I last saw you.'

As they came out of the hotel an hour later, Robyn realised that although she had told him almost everything that had happened to her over the past two years, he had told her practically nothing at all about himself, except to indicate that he had had a change of heart about his future career. Ross had always been a good listener; clever at getting people to talk about themselves. It was a valuable attribute for any doctor. But she also remembered that he found the skill useful in evading questions when the occasion arose. Why he had chosen Crownhaven and Dr Muir's practice was still a mystery, but it seemed clear that he had mellowed. He had certainly lost that fierce, all-consuming ambition of his. What could have happened to bring about this change of heart?' she wondered.

As they stood on the hotel steps he glanced down at her, then at his watch.

'Aren't you working today?'

She shook her head. 'No. It's my day off.' Her heart quickened. Was he going to ask her to have lunch with him? If he did, would she have the strength of character to refuse? Perhaps...

A car horn sounded and she saw his head turn quickly. She followed his gaze to a white sports car that had drawn up on the other side of the road. In the driving seat sat a girl with long blonde hair. She waved and Ross lifted his hand in response. He turned to her.

'It was good to see you and hear your news, Robyn,' he said. 'I expect we'll be running into each other from time to time. Good Luck.'

She watched as he walked quickly across the road. The girl wound down the window and removed the sunglasses she was wearing, revealing beautiful eyes that smiled up invitingly at Ross. He bent to kiss her lightly in greeting. Robyn looked away, hating the way her heart turned over at the sight.

The car moved off, mingling with the traffic that quickly swallowed it up, and Robyn began to walk aimlessly towards the town centre, her heart heavy inside her. Ross had said he had an appointment, but somehow she hadn't been prepared for the girl. How relieved he must be to know she did not intend to make life difficult for him! Clearly a jealous ex-lover would be a disaster in the circumstances. Well, the interview she had been dreading was over. Now they could forget it.

But as she walked, looking unseeingly into shop windows, she couldn't help speculating on the attractive girl's identity. How long had Ross known her? Maybe it was a well established relationship and he had brought her here with him. Were they perhaps engaged? What were his feelings regarding marriage these days? As a GP he would be in a completely different situation.

She shrugged impatiently. Fay was going out for the day after she had had a sleep. She would be going straight to the hospital when it was time for her to go on duty. What was she – Robyn – going to do with the rest of the day? She hesitated, her footsteps dragging as she wandered aimlessly along the street. At last she made up her mind. She would go back to Ravenshore and set about tidying the cottage garden ready for the winter. She and Fay had been meaning to do it for ages. Perhaps it wasn't the most exciting way to spend her day off, but it was guaranteed to occupy her energy and concentrate her mind.

She slept badly that night and had been up for hours by the time Fay arrived back from her night shift. The other girl looked around the spotless kitchen in surprise.

'Heavens, the place looks like a new pin! We're not expecting visitors, are we?'

Robyn laughed. 'You needn't make it sound so unusual! I do occasionally do my share, you know.' She opened the oven and took out a plate of bacon and eggs. 'Sit down and eat this breakfast I've cooked for you, though I don't know if you deserve it after that.'

Fay's eyes lit up. 'Oh, that looks wonderful.

I could eat a horse! We had quite a night on Intensive Care.' She began to tuck into the food. 'Oh, by the way, we've got your accident victim from yesterday, Daniel Rawlings.'

Robyn spun round. 'Oh, how is he?'

'Not too bad, considering,' Fay told her, tucking into her breakfast. 'It'll be a while before he's well enough to undergo the tests that will say whether he'll make a complete recovery. He might be a case for one of the big spinal units. We'll just have to wait and see. The poor lad's still pretty uncomfortable.'

Robyn sighed. 'His mother...?'

'She wanted to stay all night,' Fay told her. 'We had to insist that she went home for some rest. Daniel isn't actually on the critical list, or we could have given her a bed. I did ask Sister, as a matter of fact. I hated turning the poor woman away.'

'I'll try to look in and see him if I get time today,' said Robyn, putting on her coat. 'I shan't be able to rest until I know he's going to recover completely.'

Fay looked at her friend's pale, anxious face, her brow furrowed. 'Are you all right, Robbie? There hasn't been another development since I saw you last, has there?'

Robyn looked at her watch. 'I haven't time to talk now, but yes, there has. Ross rang after you left the night before last. Bill was here at the time, so it was rather awkward.'

'What did he want?' asked Fay. 'It must have been important for him to trace your phone number.'

'He wanted to meet and talk. I met him for coffee yesterday morning.'

'I see. What did you discover?'

Robyn pulled a face. 'Only that he still has all the same irritating ways; that he's as arrogant as ever *and* as secretive.' She looked again at her watch. 'Also that he has a glamorous new girl-friend, which was obviously the reason he wanted to see me so urgently; to make sure I wasn't going to make life difficult and embarrassing for him.' She picked up her bag. 'Damn, I'm going to be late. See you later, Fay.'

As the door slammed behind Robyn, Fay shook her head. Clearly her friend still had it badly for Dr Ross St Clair. A pity. He sounded a prize horror.

When Robyn had signed the day book that morning and changed into her uniform she found that she and Jim had been assigned to clinic duty for which they would use a 'sitting case' vehicle. They were to pick up and ferry patients to and from the hospital for outpatient treatment. Robyn was grateful for this. As well as liking the more relaxed atmosphere and enjoying getting to know the patients, it was helping her to get to know the new area she was working in. In London she had been permanently assigned to 'front line' work, being a qualified paramedic, and this was a pleasant change for her. It brought home to her how lonely many old people were, the weekly trip to hospital often being their only outing and chance to chat to others. It gave her a feeling of satisfaction, joking with them and helping to take the tension and apprehension out of what could sometimes be a traumatic day.

It was Jim's turn to drive. Their first job was to pick up a group of elderly people and take them to the day centre for occupational therapy.

'You don't look very rested, if you don't mind me saying so, love,' he remarked. 'What did you do on your day off?'

'Tidied the garden,' she told him briefly. 'At least I got some fresh air. What about you?'

He grunted. 'Same here. Madge insisted on going Christmas shopping.'

She laughed. 'But there are nine weeks to go yet!'

'That's my missis all over,' Jim grinned. 'As soon as the New Year's in she'll be out buying Easter eggs.'

After they had seen the elderly folk safely into the day centre it was time to drive out into the suburbs of Crownhaven to pick up two patients for hospital therapy. Mr Brown was recovering from a stroke and was due for a session with the speech therapist, while his neighbour, Mr Samson from the same street, was attending Outpatients to have physiotherapy after badly fracturing his arm.

Jim chatted amiably to the two elderly men about football for most of the way, leaving Robyn to her own thoughts. She was determined to go up to Intensive Care if she could snatch a minute at the hospital, to see Daniel. She was sure Jim would understand.

She was wrong. When she suggested a flying visit to the ward Jim shook his head doubtfully at her.

'You're not still agonising about the lad, are you?' he said reprovingly. 'He's in good hands and you did the best you could. You should be thinking of your next case, not your last. You know it's fatal to get too involved.'

She looked up at him appealingly. 'Just for

a minute, Jim. I only want to say hello, that's all. You're due for a coffee break. I promise I won't be long.'

He relented. 'Oh, go on, then. But it's not right, you know.'

'What isn't right?'

'Ambulancewomen with big blue eyes like yours. How you can talk about Women's Lib, I don't know. It's us men who need liberating!'

Intensive Care was on the fourth floor, and Robyn tapped on the door of Sister's office. The voice that bade her enter had a soft Irish lilt and Robyn recognised it as belonging to Sister Delaney. She opened the door and went in.

'Good morning, Sister. I was wondering how Daniel Rawlings is this morning – Fay told me he was here.'

The small, plump woman at the desk looked up with a smile. 'Oh, good morning, Robyn. Yes, Daniel is here, though he won't be for much longer. We're moving him down to Men's Surgical after lunch. He's been on a ventilator overnight. His chest injuries were giving him breathing difficulties last night, so Mr Douglas thought it best, but he's breathing unaided this morning.'

She stood up and came round the desk.

'Would you like to take a peep at him? He's still sedated, poor lad, but I'm sure he'd like to see you.'

Daniel was in the bed nearest the doors. His arm and leg were in plaster and he was still on a drip and lying flat, but in spite of this his freckled face brightened when he saw Robyn. She took his hand, pressing the fingers gently.

'Hello, Danny. They tell me you're coming along fine. I must say you look better than the last time I saw you.'

He smiled. 'That wouldn't be difficult, would it? I was hoping I'd see you again. I wanted to thank you.'

She shook her head. 'What for? I only did what I'm paid for.'

'You can't fool me. You saved my life. I wouldn't be here now if it wasn't for you – the doc told me that. Thank your lucky stars they had a woman on duty, he said. Anyone bigger wouldn't have had the right touch.'

'You don't want to believe all they tell you, Danny,' she told him dismissively. 'Here's something for when you can eat normally again.' She put the bar of chocolate, bought at the cafeteria on her way up, on his locker.

He nodded, smiling his thanks, but his eyelids drooped heavily and she could see that the strain of talking was beginning to tire him.

''Bye, Danny,' she whispered. 'Get some rest now. I'll come and see you again soon.'

She looked in on Sister Delaney on the way out. 'I'm glad he's OK. How do you rate his chances of a complete recovery?'

Sister lifted her shoulders. 'He'll be having some X-rays later this morning. Maybe they'll give us a better idea what spinal damage has been done.' She smiled. 'By the way, the GP who helped with his rescue was here a few minutes ago.'

'Dr St Clair?' Robyn felt the tell-tale colour warm her cheeks.

'That's right. I hadn't met him before. He's new, isn't he? He tells me he's with Dr Muir and partners.' Sister smiled. 'Quite a charmer. He was here to see a patient in the GP Unit in Maternity and he thought he'd look in on Danny. Nice of him, wasn't it?'

'Yes, very.' Robyn thanked Sister and left.

She was preoccupied as she walked towards the lift. Danny was not out of the wood yet. He'd obviously be fine – as long as his spinal cord wasn't damaged. If it was, just how much of the damage would have been caused by his hasty removal from the accident site? Her mind spun back eight years to another young man seriously injured in an accident – David, her brother, and her heart contracted with the reawakened anguish of the harrowing months following that accident.

Abstractedly she reached out her hand for the lift button, but another, larger one got there first, pressing the 'up' button.

'Oh, do you mind? I'm in rather a hurry and I wanted the...' She stopped as she found herself looking into Ross's steel blue eyes.

He smiled coolly. 'Good morning.'

'I – I've been to see Danny Rawlings,' she explained, then blushed. She didn't have to excuse her movements to him. What was she thinking about?

'I saw him myself earlier,' he told her. 'He seems to be coming along quite nicely.' The lift arrived and they stepped into it. Ross looked enquiringly at her as the doors closed. 'I was about to go up the canteen for a coffee. Join me?'

She shook her head. 'I'm afraid I haven't time. I used my break to visit Danny.'

'I see. Very noble of you,' he said dryly.

She shot him a look. 'It's not noble at all. I've been worried about his spine, about the way we had to pull him free. If he's paralysed...'

'The decision was mine, you can let me worry about that,' Ross said sharply.

Robyn glanced at him. So he was worried too. That was obviously why he had been to visit Danny.

'There was no other way, of course,' she conceded. 'It was the only decision possible in the circumstances. All the same…'

'It's good of you to say so.' His eyes were hard as they glared at her and she felt the hot colour burning her cheeks. She hadn't meant to sound patronising.

The lift came to a stop, the gates opened and Ross stepped out and walked away without a backward glance. Robyn stared after him, then suddenly realised with a stab of annoyance that they had been travelling upwards. Hurriedly, she pressed the ground floor button. Jim would be wondering what had happened to her. As the lift descended she seethed at Ross's sarcasm over her visit to Danny. Did he see it as some sort of weakness to worry about a patient? If he knew what she had suffered when the same thing had happened to her brother – but then she had never disclosed that episode of her life to him – or to anyone else. It was locked up tightly inside her heart – something she would rather forget.

Jim was pacing the hospital foyer impatiently when she reached the ground floor.

'I thought you'd got lost! I've just received a call from Control – there's a maternity admission case waiting. It's only down the road. We're nearest, so we'd better get going.'

In the ambulance he glanced at her. 'Well, how is he?'

Robyn stared at him, her cheeks reddening. 'Who?'

He pulled a comic face. 'Who do you think, King Kong? Yesterday's accident victim, of course.'

'Oh, Danny! He's coming along quite well. Being transferred to Men's Surgical later today. But they still don't know just how badly his spine is injured.'

'I hope you'll stop worrying about him now,' he said. 'Can't do any good, you know. Sometimes in our job you've got to be tough with yourself.'

'I do know that, Jim,' she said quietly.

After a short drive they drew up outside a block of flats and Jim switched off the engine. 'This is it – number twenty-eight. Mrs Jones. Better come with me in case I need help.'

The young woman was going into the

second stage of labour and very frightened. Robyn sat with her in the back of the ambulance while Jim drove back to the hospital as fast as he could. At one point they ran into heavy traffic and Robyn thought she might have to deliver the baby herself, but they arrived at the hospital in time. It was as the patient was being wheeled away on a trolley that the two patients they had conveyed to Outpatients arrived ready for home. Mr Samson smiled.

'Hope you haven't been bored, waiting for us all this time,' he remarked.

Over their meal that evening Fay wanted to hear more about the meeting with Ross.

'How did you discover he had a new girl-friend – did he tell you?'

'No, I saw her for myself,' Robyn told her. 'Very glamorous. Long blonde hair, driving an expensive-looking white E-type. She picked him up outside the Grand.'

Fay looked thoughtful. 'Sounds like Fiona Muir, Dr Muir's daughter.'

'Could be – that's the practice he's with. Do you know her?'

'Yes, everyone knows Fiona. She's quite a girl. She's Dr Muir's only daughter and the apple of his eye. His wife died some years ago, so she's the only family he has.'

'What's she like?' asked Robyn.

'Quite a character,' Fay admitted.

'I don't suppose she has to work, with such a doting father?' Robyn suggested.

Fay shook her head. 'Oh, she's no parasite. She's a hardworking physio, as a matter of fact. She's working at the General at the moment, but had a fabulous job taking care of an oil sheik's daughter a while ago. The child was having treatment in this country for a hip injury and Fiona travelled home to Saudi Arabia with her and stayed there until the girl was on her feet again.' Fay laughed. 'She's one of those people for whom everything seems to happen. As well as a super job and a father who dotes on her, her grandmother died and left her a fortune a couple of years ago. If she wasn't such a nice person I'd hate her!'

Robyn's heart felt like stone as she looked unsmilingly at her friend. 'And I daresay whoever marries her will stand to inherit her father's practice and everything that goes with it?'

Fay looked puzzled. 'I suppose he would. Why, you're surely not suggesting…?'

'That explains a lot,' Robyn said bitterly. 'I thought it must have been something tempting to make Ross change his career plans. And to think I thought he had mellowed! Nothing's changed after all.'

'I don't think it's fair to jump to conclusions,' Fay said quickly. 'She might not be his girl-friend at all. Perhaps she was passing and happened to see him – stopped to offer him a lift. After all, he is with her father's practice.'

Robyn shook her head impatiently. 'It's obvious. They met while Ross was in Saudi Arabia. When he realised what she had to offer he gave up his plans for a surgical career and followed her home instead. No wonder he wanted to make sure I wouldn't mess things up for him!'

'You make him sound pretty despicable,' Fay said quietly.

'Do I? I'm sorry.' Robyn turned away. 'Put it down to disappointment. When I saw him yesterday he almost convinced me he'd changed for the better, that his self-seeking, ruthless streak had gone. I might have known that people like Ross don't change.'

The ache in her heart was almost unbearable. While she was speaking she was all too aware that her words did her no credit, but she could find no others to express what she felt. Why, oh, *why* did Ross have to turn up here, just when she thought she had put him out of her thoughts – out of her heart for ever?

CHAPTER THREE

It was the following week, when Robyn was on night duty, when the accident call came. It had been a quiet night. After checking their vehicle and equipment at the beginning of the shift, she and Jim had been passing the time playing Monopoly with the other team on duty. It was after midnight when the station officer came in.

'Accident on the motorway. Two cars involved,' he said succinctly. 'Better get your skates on, Ruby Two.'

Jim and Robyn hurried outside to their waiting vehicle. It was Robyn's turn to drive and as she turned out of the yard she reached for the beacon switch; no need to use the sirens so late at night. In five minutes they were out of town and heading west on the motorway. Neither of them spoke, both were too busy watching the road ahead for signs of the accident. It was only a few minutes later that they spotted it. Ahead of them on the dual carriageway two cars had obviously collided, apparently when one was trying to overtake the other. One was already in flames, the other was dangerously close to it. Robyn pulled over on to the hard shoulder, noticing as she did so that a fire tender had already arrived and was preparing to put out the fire.

'Looks like one car has come off a lot worse than the other,' Jim remarked as he opened his door and jumped out.

Two dazed-looking people stood at the roadside, shivering from shock and the chill of the late autumn night as they bent over a third person, sitting on the grass verge. One of them, a middle-aged man, ran over to Jim and Robyn.

'Thank God you've come so quickly!' he gasped. 'There's a child in the back of the other car. We got the man out, he was unconscious, so we didn't know about the child till he came round and asked for her. When we went back we couldn't get the doors open. You'd better be quick – I reckon it could go up at any minute.'

'What about the burning car?' Jim asked him. 'Anyone in there?' The man shook his head.

'It's mine. Wife and I got out before the fire started.' He pointed to the others, a woman and the man he had rescued, now conscious, who sat head in hands on the grass verge. 'The chap seems pretty upset and the wife has a nasty cut on her forehead.'

Jim turned to Robyn. 'Go and have a quick look at them while I get a crowbar. The heat from the fire will have jammed the doors of the car,' he said. 'There isn't any time to lose. Chances are it'll go up any minute.'

Robyn examined the other passengers quickly. They had been lucky, sustaining only cuts and bruises, although she suspected that the father of the child had concussion. He still seemed dazed and shocked and kept asking over and over for his small daughter, whose name was Julie. Reassuring them as best she could, Robyn helped them into the ambulance and then hurried over to where Jim was still struggling with the car doors. All four were jammed tight.

'Nothing for it but to break the rear windscreen and try to get the kid out,' he said. 'I can't see in, the windows are too misted, so I don't know how old she is, but a few scratches will be better than being fried alive. Stand back!'

There was a crash as the rear windscreen shattered under the impact of the crowbar and Robyn helped him to push out the granulated glass. Climbing on to the car boot, Robyn peered in through the aperture. At first she could see nothing, then, pulling aside a man's coat that lay across the back seat, she uncovered a baby, about a year old, asleep in a carrycot. Scooping her up, she handed her safely out to Jim and then scrambled out on to the road as firemen began to spray the car with fire extinguishers.

'A bit of luck,' she told Jim breathlessly. 'The man must have hung his coat in the back, and it fell over the child. She didn't even wake up, and there doesn't seem to be a scratch on her.'

At the hospital the man and his small daughter were admitted. The occupants of the other car were treated for shock and allowed home after the woman's forehead had been stitched. Jim fetched Robyn a cup of coffee from the machine in Accident and Emergency.

'I wonder if those two jammy beggars back at Control have finished the game of Monopoly without us?' he mused.

It was Robyn's last night on a night shift. The following day she was free, and she had already made plans to visit Danny Rawlings at the hospital. Since he had been moved to

Men's Surgical she had heard no more news of him and she was anxious to check on his progress.

She found him much improved, but he was not alone. At his bedside sat a small, slim woman whom Danny introduced as his mother. She stood up and took the hand Robyn held out in both of hers, holding it warmly.

'I'm so glad to meet you, my dear. I've been wanting to thank you for saving Danny's life,' she said. Robyn shook her head.

'Please,' she muttered, 'I only did my job. How is he? Have you had the results of any of the tests yet?'

'They don't think his spinal cord is damaged,' Mrs Rawlings told her. 'He still has no sensation or use in his legs, but they say it could be due to injury to the nerves. We shall just have to wait and see.' She smiled at her son. 'The main thing is, he's all right. I can cope with anything as long as I've still got him.'

As Robyn came down from the ward in the lift she was deep in thought. It seemed it was going to be a long job for Danny. She wondered how he would cope with his disability and whether his mother's concern for him might be somewhat stifling. If only there were something she could do to help!

As she crossed the entrance lobby she was so deep in thought that she didn't see Bill coming towards her.

'Well, tuppence to speak to you today, is it?'

Startled, she looked up. 'Oh – sorry, Bill, I didn't see you.' She frowned. 'What are you doing here anyway? This is off your usual beat, isn't it?'

'Ah, my eager newshound's nose caught the scent of a juicy story!' He tapped the side of his nose. 'A tug-of-love case – father running off with his small daughter. Would have made it too if he hadn't been involved in an accident on the way to the airport.'

Robyn's eyes widened. 'Not the motorway crash last night? A man with a little girl about a year old?'

'That's the one. Usual thing – couple divorced, father didn't think his wife suitable for custody even though the judge did...'

Robyn stared at him. 'You haven't been up to the ward, trying to get a story?' she asked.

He pursed his lips. 'Nothing doing at the moment – Sister's a bit of an old dragon.' He grinned. 'But the staff nurse let it slip that she'd be going for a tea break at four, so I'm hanging around till then.' He glanced at his watch. 'It seems the guy will probably be discharged tomorrow and I don't want to risk somebody else getting in with the story first.'

'Don't you think it's a bit much, harassing him like that?' said Robyn disapprovingly. 'The poor man has enough to handle at the moment, I'd have thought.'

Bill grinned. 'There's something else. I happen to know through a mate of mine in the police that the child's mother is on her way here. Now if I should happen to be around...'

Robyn stared at him. 'You wouldn't! Are you seriously telling me that you'd intrude on something as private as that?'

'You're kidding, love, it's my job.' He looked at her in surprise. 'I thought you understood.'

Robyn shook her head, starting to walk towards the main entrance. 'Somehow I didn't connect you with that kind of behaviour, Bill,' she said. 'Not on a small town newspaper.'

Bill followed her. 'Look, don't go like that. Everyone has to do their job, and sometimes it entails things that are unpleasant. Heavens above, you of all people should know that!'

She opened her mouth to say something,

but stopped as she saw a tall, purposeful figure bearing down on them. 'Oh!'

Bill turned to follow her gaze just as Ross caught up with them.

'Are you the reporter from the *Courier?*'

Bill nodded, taken aback by the fierce expression on this total stranger's face.

'Yes, that's right.'

Ross took his arm and propelled him towards the doors. 'Can we have a word – in private?'

Robyn followed them out into the car park. Ross was clearly very angry and she guessed that he had heard about Bill's visit to the men's medical ward. In the comparative privacy of the car park Ross gave vent to his fury.

'I understand you've been harassing the Sister and staff on Men's Medical,' he said, his eyes steely under drawn brows. 'If I hear you've been here again on your grubby little muck-raking quest, I shall remove you personally. Is that clear?'

Bill drew himself up to his full height and looked Ross in the eye. 'And just who do you think *you* are?' he demanded. 'I've never set eyes on you before.'

'I happen to be a doctor in this town,' Ross told him stiffly. 'I was visiting a patient at the hospital when I heard of your disgraceful behaviour.'

Robyn stepped forward, feeling she should intervene. If Bill lost his temper too there was no telling what might happen. 'Ross, this is Bill Hughes,' she said. 'He's a reporter on the *Courier...*' She trailed off lamely as Ross stared at her coldly as though noticing her for the first time.

'What has this to do with you?'

Before she could reply Bill jumped in: 'This young lady happens to be the ambulance-woman who brought the accident victims to the hospital last night,' he explained. 'She also happens to be...' He hesitated, moistening his lips before finishing the sentence: 'the girl I intend to marry.'

There was a moment's silence as the three stared at each other. Robyn was stunned. Why on earth had Bill said that? She was aware of Ross's eyes on her and looked up to meet their icy glare.

'I see! That makes everything crystal clear.' He turned back to Bill. 'I can understand *your* lack of ethics, Hughes – from my experience of newspaper reporters they don't know the meaning of the word. But I would have thought that a member of the ambulance service would have had more integrity than to blab to the press!'

Robyn stared from one to the other, too appalled to speak. Bill put in:

'It wasn't Robbie – she didn't tell me anything. I just happened to meet her and...'

But Ross was already turning away. 'Remember what I said, Hughes,' he warned. 'If I even hear that you've been hanging around here again...'

He strode across to where a black Jaguar X was parked and got in. Bill snorted.

'Look at that! I might have known he'd have a car like that. All image, these types. I wonder how he'd like someone to tell him how to do *his* job?'

'Why on earth did you tell him that lie?' demanded Robyn. 'You really do have a nerve, Bill! He'll obviously think now that I'm giving you information about patients!'

Bill took her arm. 'Sorry, love. I don't know what made me say it – impulse, I suppose. I just wanted to knock that pompous look off his face.' He looked down at her, his face apologetic. 'I didn't mean to land you in the soup. Anyway, let him think what he likes, interfering nerk! Who cares anyway?' He looked at his watch again. 'Oh, look, it's gone four. I'll have to hurry if I want to get up there before Sister gets back.'

'You're not still going through with it after what Ross said?' Robyn asked.

Bill laughed. 'I've been threatened by bigger blokes than him. Little episodes like that are all in a day's work. Helps to keep the old adrenalin flowing!' He began to walk away, then looked back thoughtfully at her over his shoulder. 'By the way, remind me to ask you how you knew his name some time, will you?'

Before she could say another word he was out of earshot, racing back towards the hospital entrance, the ends of his old scarf flying. She stared after his hurrying figure, biting her lip with impotent fury. *She* cared what Ross thought – and not just because of their past relationship. No one in her position would relish being accused of acting in an unethical way. How typical of Bill not to see that! And how typical of Ross to jump to such a conclusion.

For a moment she considered the contrast between the two men as they had faced each other; Ross so well groomed in his immaculate dark suit and Bill in his scruffy old tweed jacket and scarf, his fair hair tousled and badly needing the attention of a barber. The two men were poles apart in every way. Perhaps that was why Bill had attracted her.

Shrugging, she turned towards her own car, feeling in the pocket of her coat for her keys.

She was just getting in when she heard a voice calling and looked up to see Danny Rawlings' mother waving to her.

'Miss – er – please wait.' The woman was slightly breathless as she came up to the car. 'I'm sorry, I don't know your name. I wondered if we might have a word?'

Robyn held out her hand. 'Robyn Seers. I'm sorry, I should have introduced myself back at the hospital.' She looked at the older woman's anxious face and asked: 'There's nothing wrong, is there?'

'No – at least...' Mrs Rawlings hesitated, then asked, 'Look, I don't suppose you have time for a cup of tea, do you? I would like to talk to you.'

The visitors' cafeteria in the hospital was quiet and they took their tea to a corner table. Mrs Rawlings lit a cigarette, offering the packet to Robyn, who shook her head. As she pushed it back into her handbag the other woman smiled apologetically.

'I know it's bad for you. I did give it up a few months ago, but since Danny...'

'I know. You must have been under a terrible strain, facing it on your own.' Robyn sighed. 'If there's anything I can do...'

Mrs Rawlings looked at her sharply. 'I wondered if there was anything I should know.'

Robyn frowned. 'About what?'

The other woman looked uncomfortable. 'About Danny's accident. You seem so concerned. I wondered...' she glanced up, biting her lip, 'well, if it might have been caused by some kind of negligence. Whether there's anything I should know.'

Robyn winced inwardly. Quite clearly this was the kind of thing one risked when one became too involved with a patient. Mrs Rawlings must be wondering whether she could claim and whether Robyn might have some information that might help the case. She would have to disappoint her.

'I'm sorry,' she said. 'From what we could see when we arrived it was a pure accident, though obviously if Danny is disabled by it he will get compensation. I'm afraid my interest is purely personal.'

Mrs Rawlings looked up. 'Oh, you knew Danny before the accident, then? He never said.'

'No.' Robyn took a deep breath. It was no use, she was going to have to explain – to tell the woman about the tragedy in her own life – something she hated to talk about. 'Danny touched my heart,' she began. 'You see, my brother had an accident some years ago. It left him paraplegic – paralysed from the waist down. I always felt it was my fault – he was driving me home from a party when it happened, you see. It was a shattering experience for all of us, but more especially for David and his wife. Somehow Danny's accident brought it all back.'

Mrs Rawlings reached out to touch her hand. 'You say you were with him. Weren't you hurt at all?'

Robyn shook her head. 'No, hardly a scratch. I managed to get him out, but I always felt that if I had known more about first aid I might have saved his spine from damage. That was partly what made me go into the ambulance service.'

The other woman smiled. 'Then some good came out of it.'

Robyn smiled and nodded. Danny's mother couldn't know that there was more to it than that – far more; couldn't know, for instance, about the bitter split it had caused in her family. When she had announced that she was leaving to begin her ambulance service training in London, her sister-in-law Mary had made no secret of the fact that she considered Robyn responsible for

David's accident and that it was her duty to stay and help look after him. Inwardly Robyn recoiled as she remembered the look of bitter resentment on her face as she lashed out at her:

'*So you're opting out – leaving us to it, are you? David and I have shared our home with you, seen you through your education, and now that you've landed us in this God-awful mess you're leaving! Well, don't expect a welcome here again. Just don't come back – ever! Do you hear?*'

'You obviously made the right choice. I can see that you're very dedicated to your work.'

Robyn looked up, suddenly aware that the woman was speaking to her. 'Oh, I love my job, yes, but even if I hadn't left to train for this I'd have left. I lived with my brother and his wife, you see. I'd been with them since our parents died. David was twelve years older than me. They'd been good to me. But after David's accident I could see it all falling apart. I knew that if I didn't leave, Mary probably would. She wasn't adjusting at all well to David's disability, and I didn't want to be the cause of his marriage breaking up too...'

Mrs Rawlings squeezed Robyn's fingers.

'You poor child, how awful for you!'

Robyn smiled apologetically. 'I'm only telling you so that you'll understand why I felt so sorry for Danny. I don't usually talk about it. In fact you're the first person I've mentioned David to for ages.'

The other woman smiled gently. 'It helps sometimes to talk, especially to a stranger. How is your brother now?'

Robyn smiled. 'Oh, doing quite well, thanks.' How could she tell this woman that she hadn't the faintest idea how her brother was? That the letters she had written when she first moved to London had been returned unopened; the Christmas cards she always sent, never reciprocated? Clearly Mary had meant what she had said; she intended to keep Robyn out of their lives for good. She hurriedly looked at her watch and muttered an excuse to go. She felt awkward. It was the first time she had talked about David and the family split for years. No one here even knew she had a brother. She had never even told Ross. Talking about David now had opened the wound anew and she didn't agree that it did one good to talk; not even to a stranger. She stood up, pulling on her gloves.

'I'd like to come and see Danny again, if I

may,' she said. 'But please say if you'd rather I didn't.'

Mrs Rawlings smiled. 'I'd love you to visit him. We don't have many friends and people aren't keen to visit hospitals. Danny may be moved, of course, but they could send him to the spinal unit at Ennermoor. That wouldn't be too far to go.'

Robyn felt low as she drove back to Ravenshore. What had become of David? she wondered. Were he and Mary still together? Maybe he needed her. Maybe she should try to find out whether he really was at the old address and if not where he had moved to. She was still deep in thought when she drew up outside the cottage, so deep in thought that at first she failed to see the sleek black car already parked outside until she got out of her own car and began to walk towards the gate. Seeing her, the driver got out and Robyn realised with a shock that it was Ross. Her fingers trembled as they fumbled with the door key.

'I thought you'd never come!' he said as he joined her in the porch.

She glanced at him. 'Well, I'm sorry if you've had a long wait. If I'd known...' She pushed open the door. 'I suppose you want to come in,' she added ungraciously. He still looked angry, and the last thing she wanted at this moment was a sermon.

'I would rather like to speak to you, and I take it you'd prefer it not to be on the doorstep,' he said tersely.

'If you really want to know I'd prefer it to be not at all, but if you must, you'd better come in.' She went inside and closed the door after him. Taking off her outdoor things, she looked up at him.

'You'd better come through into the living-room.' She opened the door and stood aside for him to pass. He looked around the little room approvingly, noting the low, beamed ceiling and the stone fireplace flanked by bookshelves; the comfortable chintz-covered settee and chairs.

'Very nice.'

Robyn ignored the remark. 'What can I do for you?' she asked, looking pointedly at her watch. 'Or perhaps it would save time if I were to tell you! You've come to tell me how badly I've behaved in giving information to a newspaper reporter – possibly even that you don't care for the company I keep! Well, let me tell you before you start that I have never at any time given information about patients to Bill Hughes or anyone else. And as for the company I keep, that's entirely my own affair!'

Ross looked down at her, one eyebrow raised in the indolent way she had always found infuriating. 'Well, I hope you feel better after that little outburst! I see you haven't changed, Robyn. You still have that chip on your shoulder. As it happens, I came to give you a friendly warning.'

'Warning? About what?'

'About the kind of people you mix with. You were right about that part of it at least – I never for a moment thought that you'd given information to that scruffy little nobody from the local rag. I thought you had better taste than to have your name linked with his, though.'

Robyn felt her colour rise as she said hotly: 'And what makes *you* qualified to judge, may I ask?'

He laughed. 'Really, Robyn! One has only to look at him. Of course I realise that he took you by surprise when he came out with the bit about your being the girl he intended to marry.'

'Oh, you did, did you? Well, let me tell you that it happens to be the truth!' The moment she had said the words she wished she could take them back. There was a stunned silence as Ross stared at her, then, feeling she had to say something defensive, she added: 'Some of us are driven by motives other than mercenary ones, you know. Some of us are interested in people for themselves and not just what we stand to gain by the alliance!'

He took a step towards her, his eyes narrowing. 'And just what does that mean?'

He was standing very close to her, so close that she had to tip her head back to look up at him. She felt at a disadvantage, backing away till she felt the coffee table against the backs of her legs. 'I don't care to go into it further,' she said shakily. She began to edge sideways round the table, but his hands shot out to grasp her shoulders.

'Keep still, damn it!' he snapped. 'Now, you'll just explain that last remark, if you please. You can't make snide remarks like that and then just sheer off.'

Robyn took a deep breath. 'Look, a long time ago I realised that we wanted different things from life, Ross. You choose your friends and I'll choose mine. Let's just leave it at that. It doesn't matter to me what you do and I don't see why my affairs should bother you.'

His eyes were enigmatic as they looked down into hers. 'But they do, Robyn,' he said quietly. 'Your "affairs", as you call them, bother me very much. I feel responsible for you. It's impossible not to, having shared my life with you for a whole year. I can't pretend to understand your reason for walking out on me the way you did, and as you say, our relationship was over long ago, but still, I can't stand by and watch you making a fool of yourself.'

She gasped. 'How can you be such a hypocrite? How dare you – you...'

He shook her slightly.

'Don't let's get emotional about it. As you've already said, there's nothing to be gained by dragging it all up again. It's just that I feel it may have clouded your judgement – given you a false set of values.'

She stared up at him coldly. 'Are you saying that I'm on the rebound?'

He shrugged. 'I suppose that is one way of putting it.'

'*Oh!*' She shook herself free of his restraining hands and walked to the door. 'I've always known you were arrogant,' she snapped, turning in the doorway. 'Arrogant and high-handed, but this takes the biscuit! As you said the other day, we're adult, responsible people. If we have to live and work in the same town we're both going to have to learn to keep out of each other's hair.'

Ross smiled. 'Did I really say that?'

'That was the gist of it, but you're not making it very easy!'

He crossed to the doorway where she stood and quite deliberately closed the door. 'I'll let you know when I'm ready to leave, Robyn,' he said quietly. 'Now, to continue: I think my memory is a little more reliable than yours and I seem to remember you saying you had formed another relationship. Am I to take it that this – this Hughes is the man in question?'

'Correct! How many more times do you need telling?' She looked up at him defiantly. Her heart was beating uncomfortably fast as he stood towering over her. She would have liked to move away, but she felt she would lose ground if she did. Did he guess at the effect his nearness was having on her? Her heart sank as she realised that the chemistry between them was as strong as ever. Fighting down the urge to fall into his arms and melt against him, she said:

'Any objections – other than superficial ones?' She took an involuntary step backwards as he leaned towards her.

'I don't like seeing you throw yourself away.'

'Then don't look!' Her voice was thin and

brittle and she tried to take a deep breath, but her chest was too constricted. 'You've got a nerve,' she told him. 'Coming here and telling me who I should go out with after what you did. Please go!' She reached out her hand to the door handle, but he caught it, holding it fast.

'What did I do, Robyn?' His eyes burned into hers.

She shook her head, turning away. Why was he torturing her like this? Why wouldn't he just go and leave her alone? What a fool she had been to imagine they could live and work in the same town and behave as though nothing had happened. She swallowed hard, dangerously close to tears.

Still holding her wrist, Ross lifted her chin with his other hand, forcing her to look at him. The blue eyes were dark as they searched hers.

'Why are you so upset?'

She opened her mouth, but the words she wanted to say simply refused to come. To her dismay she felt a tear overflow and slide down her cheek. 'Damn you, Ross!' she managed to gasp. 'Why did you have to choose this place? Why can't you leave me alone? I hate you, do you hear?' But it was no use; the words came out in an ineffectual squeak and Ross ignored them as his arms went round her. For a moment she struggled feebly, hammering her fists against his chest, but he held her fast until she gave in, leaning her forehead against his shoulder, breathing in the achingly familiar scent of him, her heart swelling as though it would burst.

'Here...' He pushed a handkerchief into the clenched fist still pressed against his chest. 'I don't suppose you've got one of your own. You never had!'

She dabbed at her cheeks with it. Looking up at him, she started to say something – make some sort of confused apology, but before the words had time to reach her lips his hand cupped her chin firmly and his mouth came down on hers.

The fire inside her flared up anew as he rekindled all that she had spent the past months trying to quench. No one else would ever have the power to make her feel like this. Knees weak, she clung to him, responding to the kiss with all the desperate longing she had stifled for so long. Shutting out the warning signals that rang inside her head, she existed only for that moment. She had the curious sensation of swinging on a silken thread, suspended in time. But that thread was snapped rudely as the front doorbell suddenly rang out.

For a moment they stared at each other, Ross's arms dropped to his sides.

'You'd better answer it.'

Robyn turned and went into the hall. Bill stood on the step, smiling at her.

'Hi – are you ready?'

She stared back at him numbly. 'Ready – for what?'

The smile left his face. 'You haven't forgotten that we have a date? It's your day off, remember?'

'Oh – no, of course not.' She was aware that Bill was looking past her into the hall and turned to see Ross standing there.

'I'll go, then,' he said. 'I'm sorry if I've taken up too much of your time.'

There was nothing she could do but let him go, and she watched helplessly as he walked to his car and got in without a backward glance. Bill walked past her into the hall.

'What did old pompous-pants want?'

She turned. 'Want? Oh, nothing – just to check on something,' she said abstractedly.

'Well, never mind, he's gone, that's the main thing.' He grabbed her and swung her round. 'Go and get your glad rags on. We've got some celebrating to do. I've just scooped the story of my career!'

89

CHAPTER FOUR

Robyn was silent in the car. While Bill chattered on about his story her mind was full of the conversation she had had with Ross. She still didn't understand it. Surely he hadn't driven all the way out to Ravenshore just to tell her she was going out with the wrong man? Why should he concern himself when he had a new girl-friend himself? How dared he presume he still had the right to dictate to her? Then there was the kiss. Had her tears affected him, or was he just trying to prove something? She squirmed inwardly, remembering the way she had responded, and her stomach churned at the memory of the havoc it had caused. It had been like stirring up an emotional wasps' nest and she was still suffering from the stings!

'Anything wrong, love?' Bill had stopped the car and was leaning forward to peer into her face.

She shook herself slightly as though trying to rid herself of the memory. 'No – nothing.'

'That St Clair didn't upset you, did he?'

'Of course not.'

'By the way, that reminds me, how *did* you know his Christian name?'

'I trained at the same hospital in London, that's all. Look, shall we stop talking about him now?'

'Sure.' Bill grinned at her. 'Well, what do you think of my scoop, then? Bill Hughes, ace reporter, eh?' He took in her blank expression and sighed. 'There, I knew you hadn't heard a word I'd said! Might as well talk to the wall!'

'Sorry, Bill. Tell me again.'

'It was the couple with the baby,' he repeated patiently. 'It turned out they weren't divorced, just separated. He was cut up about being parted from the child – well, from both of them, as it happens – and he'd snatched the child while she was being looked after by a baby-sitter. I told you I'd found out that the wife was on her way to the hospital? She arrived soon after you'd left.' He grinned. 'It was just like something from one of those soap operas. You should have been there! All the nurses were in tears! They made it up on the spot. When she saw him with his head bandaged she just melted! Anyway, being on the scene, secreted behind a bowl of grapes, as it were, I got an exclusive on it.' He leaned back, half closing his eyes. 'Can't you just see that headline? *Near-tragedy has happy ending– Couple reconciled over child's hospital bed.* What do you think, eh?'

'Very dramatic. Congratulations.'

'And you don't think I'm a hardbitten newshound any more, eh?'

'No. You're an angel in disguise.' Robyn smiled. 'Mind you, sometimes it's a very *good* disguise!'

Bill slipped an arm round her shoulders. 'My editor liked it anyway, that's the main thing. It's a change to be in his good books. Now, where would you like to go – disco – film – pub? Maybe we can even get tickets for the theatre in Crownhaven if we try.'

Robyn shook her head. 'If you don't mind, Bill, I'd rather just go somewhere for a quiet meal.'

He gave her shoulders a squeeze. 'Ah, soft lights, romantic music and an intimate table for two, eh? Couldn't agree more. I know just the place.'

He started the car again and Robyn sighed. Oh dear, now she'd given Bill the wrong impression too!

The evening was a dismal failure. Although

she tried hard to enjoy herself, Robyn couldn't keep her mind off Ross and his visit to the cottage earlier. Bill had to repeat almost everything he said. He didn't complain, just teased her about her absentmindedness, which made her feel worse. He was so nice and he had gone to endless trouble to give her an enjoyable evening. She felt so mean to be spoiling his moment of glory. At last she said so.

'I'm sorry, Bill, I must be tired or something, though goodness knows why on my day off. Have I ruined your evening?'

He shook his head, reaching for her hand across the table. 'Of course you haven't. Just being with you is enough for me.' He looked at his watch. 'Look, tell you what, let's go back to the flat for coffee, shall we? You can relax more there.' He looked at her shrewdly. 'And if there's anything bothering you, you can talk about it – if you want to, that is.'

Bill's flat was really no more than a glorified bed-sit. It was in a small back street on the fringes of Crownhaven, but he had made it cosy, decorating it brightly with brilliant travel posters covering the drab wallpaper. He lit the gas fire and filled the kettle in the curtained-off corner he called his kitchen.

'I've got some of those chocolate biscuits you like,' he told her over his shoulder. 'You know, the wafer ones.'

Robyn sank down on the settee that converted into a bed. 'I don't think I could eat another thing, thanks.' Then, seeing his face, she added, 'Well, maybe just one, then.'

Bill deposited the coffee tray on the table in front of her and put on a record that he knew she liked, Spanish music played by a well known guitarist.

'There, the next best thing to sunshine,' he told her with a smile. Inwardly she shrank. If only he would tell her not to be such a misery – lose his temper – anything but this awful tolerance. She poured the coffee, wondering what to say, feeling she owed him an explanation, but before she had time to think of one he said:

'I've been thinking. I've got some time off due to me. Why don't we go away for a few days – just the two of us? You've never explored the Lakeland countryside properly and I'd love to show it to you. It can be so beautiful at this time of year, before the winter sets in.'

Robyn looked at his hopeful face and didn't have the heart to refuse outright.

'That could be fun,' she said, trying hard to sound enthusiastic. 'I don't know when I could manage it, though.'

'You would like it, though?'

'Yes, it sounds a lovely idea.'

Bill smiled happily and slipped an arm round her shoulders, pulling her close until her head rested on his shoulder. 'Know something?' He sighed. 'I'd rather be here with you like this than anywhere else on earth at this moment.' He bent his head to brush his lips across hers, then, drawing her close, he kissed her, gently at first, then with more urgency, his arms tightening round her.

Suddenly she was filled with a wild, unreasonable panic; all kinds of emotions running through her. Since Ross had kissed her again earlier this evening she knew it was no use pretending. She was still as much in love with him as ever; there was no denying it. All the months of trying to forget him had been swept aside with that one kiss. She felt angry. He didn't care tuppence for her; didn't know the meaning of love in the sweet, gentle way that Bill did. Why couldn't she fall for a man who would love her as she wanted to be loved? But it was no use; try as she would she couldn't respond to Bill and it wasn't fair to him to pretend. Pushing him away, she leapt to her feet, her heart hammering.

'No! I'm sorry, Bill, I can't…' She stood with her back to him, fighting back the tears. There was a moment's silence, then he said quietly:

'It isn't just tiredness, is it, Robbie? Please tell me what's wrong. I'm not going to throw a fit if you say there's someone else.'

She heard him move and felt his hands gently touch her shoulders. Turning, she looked into his eyes.

'Oh, Bill! There was someone else – you knew that. There isn't any more. It's just – just that I'm not as over it as I thought. I still need time.'

He bent and kissed her forehead. 'Well, if that's all there's no problem.'

She sighed deeply. If only he were right! It was going to take a lot more time than even Bill would be prepared to wait – a *whole* lot more.

It was the following day at lunch that Fay told her about the party. Still preoccupied, Robyn was only half listening until the other girl's expression told her that she was required to give an answer. She looked up at

Fay's enquiring face.

'Sorry. What did you say?'

Fay shook her head. 'Honestly! I don't know what's the matter with you lately. I've been telling you at some length about this party at Fiona Muir's and you haven't heard a word I've said!'

'I'm sorry, I think I'm half asleep. Still catching up after my stint on night duty. It always affects me like that.'

'Night duty nothing!' Fay said bluntly. 'You've been like this ever since Dr Ross St Clair reappeared on your scene! It's just that you're even worse today. Has anything happened that I haven't heard about?'

'Of course not. You were saying about this party,' said Robyn, changing the subject. 'It sounds interesting. At Fiona Muir's, you say?'

'That's right.' Fay stared at her. 'Well, can you go?'

'But why should she invite me? She doesn't even know me.'

'I've been telling you that,' Fay told her. 'She knows I share a cottage and she invited me and my friend – that's you, in case you've forgotten!' she smiled. 'She also said to bring a couple of boy-friends. Will you ask Bill? I'm sure he'd love it.'

'I'll have to check that we're neither of us working that night,' Robyn said.

It happened that both of them were free, so it was arranged that they should go in a foursome along with Fay's boy-friend, Alan. Robyn was a little apprehensive. Would Ross be there? Unless he was on call it was likely. After all, he was Fiona's current escort. As the evening approached she grew nervous.

On the Saturday before the party the two girls went shopping. Fay had decided to treat herself to a new dress and had persuaded Robyn to buy one too.

'After all, it is the beginning of the party season and there's Christmas coming up too,' she said enthusiastically as they travelled into Crownhaven in Robyn's car. 'By the way, what do you plan to do for Christmas, go home?'

Robyn shook her head. It was a season she had dreaded since her break with David and Mary. The two Christmases that she and Ross were together had been wonderful, but she tried not to remember them now.

'This is my only home,' she said.

Fay winced. 'Damn, I forgot! Sorry, love. But it's your fault, you know. You never talk about yourself or your background.' She patted Robyn's shoulder. 'I only wish you would confide a bit more.' She smiled. 'Don't worry, I wouldn't mind betting that Bill has something up his sleeve for this year, and if he hasn't you can always come home with me. For once I'm off duty for the holiday.'

They parked the car and set off on their shopping expedition, stopping to look in the window of Crownhaven's largest department store. Fay sighed over a ball gown of floating chiffon in shades of pink and lilac.

'Oh, look! Wouldn't it be lovely to be able to lash out on something like that? The dress I buy will have to be a little more versatile.'

They went inside to see what was on offer and eventually both found something to suit them. Robyn wanted to buy a simple black dress she thought would be useful for other occasions, but Fay persuaded her to choose instead a dress of flame-coloured chiffon. It fitted her perfectly, its full skirt swirling romantically about her hips while the vibrant flame shade did wonderful things for her colouring, bringing out the chestnut lights in her dark hair and giving a glow to her creamy complexion.

'You'll knock 'em dead in that!' Fay told her enthusiastically. 'I only wish I could wear that colour, but it would simply make me look washed out.'

Robyn hesitated, looking wistfully at the dress. 'I don't know. It seems so extravagant. The black would be so much more useful.'

'Oh well, if you want to merge into the wallpaper...' Fay picked up the dress and held it temptingly against Robyn as the two looked into the fitting room mirror. 'Go on, Robbie, be a devil for once. I can promise you that Fiona will spare no expense to look fabulous for the party.'

'It's all right for her. She doesn't have to count the pennies,' Robyn protested. Nevertheless she finally succumbed to her friend's persuasion and bought the dress, trying to ignore the wicked inner voice that persisted in reminding her that red was Ross's favourite colour.

There was a week to go until the party and it was an especially busy week at the Control Centre. The weather, which until now had been pleasant and mild, suddenly turned wet and bitterly cold. Greasy roads led to the usual spate of minor accidents and several elderly people developed bronchitis and had to be taken into hospital for treatment.

The day before the party was fraught with problems. When Robyn arrived at Control she found that Jim hadn't signed on for the shift. His wife telephoned to say he had developed flu. Robyn was teamed with another partner, John Foster, and asked to split the shift following hers, which meant that she had to get a message to Fay to say she wouldn't be home to supper.

All day they were busy; two maternity cases, a worker at the local engineering factory who had received a bad electric shock. An old lady who had collapsed and lain unattended for hours until a neighbour had found her.

Robyn and John snatched a quick snack and began their split shift with a call to a child with asthma. As she edged the ambulance out of the station yard Robyn sighed. It was dinner time and she was unable to erase the image of Fay at Fell Cottage, cooking the steak and kidney pie she had promised to make tonight, one of her specialities.

The small boy lying on the settee in the neat living-room was about eight years old and in quite a bad way when they arrived. His mother was distraught.

'He's had a bad cold, and that always starts off his asthma, but he's never been as bad as this before,' she told them anxiously. 'He

102

terrified me when he couldn't get his breath. I've already rung the doctor, but when he hadn't arrived after half an hour, and when Ricky seemed to lose consciousness, I got worried and dialled 999.'

'How long has he been like this?' Robyn had already dropped to her knees beside the little boy on the settee, nothing his bluish colour and lifeless appearance.

'It seems like ages. I thought help would never come. He's not…? Oh God! Is there anything I can do?'

Robyn put her fingers against the carotid artery in his neck. There was no beat. She moved him quickly to the floor, glancing up at the mother, whose face was white and strained.

'Perhaps you should ring the surgery again, to see what's holding the doctor up.'

Urgently she began mouth-to-mouth resuscitation while John went out to the ambulance for an emergency oxygen pack. Alternating breaths and cardiac compression, Robyn worked steadily and by the time John returned with the oxygen she had the boy's heart beating again. She looked up at John as she held the mask to the child's face.

'Better radio the hospital. I think he should go in for observation.' She gave her attention to the child once more, turning him into the recovery position and watching with relief as his colour returned. There was a movement in the doorway and she looked up.

'The doctor's here now.' The child's mother, still looking anxious, stood to one side to admit him, and Robyn's heart gave a jerk when she saw that it was Ross.

'What kept you?' she muttered angrily at him when they were alone. 'It was a good job we came when we did. Another couple of minutes and this child would have been dead!' She glared up at him, not caring or thinking about her words, or his reaction to them. Children always affected her. They were so vulnerable; so fragile and dependent. How could anyone neglect an emergency call to one?

Ross's face was hard and expressionless as he eased her out of the way.

'You'd better let me see him.' Taking out his stethoscope, he made a brief examination, then turned to her. 'He's in shock, but he'll be all right. I'd like him admitted to hospital for observation, though. You'd better take him straight away now that you're here.'

'I've already sent word that we're on our way,' she told him shortly.

John appeared in the doorway carrying the warmed blanket always ready in the ambulance, and the child was wrapped up and carried out to the vehicle while his mother put on her coat and prepared to go with them.

Robyn watched Ross's car drive away as she started the engine. John looked up from writing his report.

'Sick, isn't it? The things some people do for kicks!'

Robyn glanced at him. 'Sorry?'

'The call,' he explained. 'The one that delayed the doctor. He told me briefly about it. He had a radio call when he was on his way here. A woman was supposed to have taken an overdose at the high-rise flats in Meredith Street. Lift was out of order, as usual, and he'd legged it all the way up to the tenth floor before he discovered there was no such person. It was a hoax call.'

Robyn felt her face turning crimson. 'I didn't know,' she muttered. 'I'm afraid I was a bit outspoken when he turned up.'

John grinned. 'I thought you'd said something, by the look on both your faces. Kids always get to you girls, don't they?'

Robyn bit her lip, John's sexist remark going over her head. 'I suppose I shall have to apologise,' she said ruefully.

'Let that be a lesson to you. Never jump to conclusions,' he told her with a grin.

Fay's boy-friend Alan was to arrive at eight the following evening to take both girls to the party. At the last minute Bill's paper had sent him to cover an away match of the local football team and he didn't expect to arrive back in Crownhaven until later. He was going straight on to the party and meeting Robyn there. It had been the final snag in a trying week. She would have preferred to arrive with Bill. The events of the past week had left her feeling limp and for once she felt in need of some moral support.

As the girls waited for Alan, Fay glanced at Robyn. Her hair newly shampooed and brushed into a shining halo of curls, set off by the new dress and just the right amount of make-up, she made quite a picture, in spite of her obvious misgivings.

'Cheer up, you look marvellous,' Fay said reassuringly. 'That dress was a good buy. You did right to get it.' When she received little reaction she shook her head. 'Well, don't you agree?'

'What? Oh yes, I suppose so.' A car drew up outside and Robyn got to her feet, looking at Fay apprehensively. 'Look, I don't think I'll come after all. Bill probably won't make it and I'll feel awkward on my own. Fiona doesn't know me, so she won't mind. You'll make my apologies, won't you?'

'I'll do nothing of the kind!' Fay frowned. 'What *is* the matter, Robbie? I wish you'd tell me. You've been bothered about something ever since you got home last night.'

Robyn hesitated, then explained her angry outburst to Ross over the asthmatic child. Fay smiled.

'You do take things to heart so! He won't hold that against you, I'm sure, especially as he knows you so well.'

'But don't you see, that's just *it!*' Robyn sank on to a chair. 'I wouldn't have said it to any other doctor. This past relationship of ours is getting in the way of work, just as I knew it would. I lost my temper...'

'Then you'll have to learn not to, won't you?' The doorbell rang and Fay went to answer it, throwing Robyn's coat at her as she went.

'Here, put that on and don't let's have any more nonsense about not coming!'

Fiona lived with her father at the Muirs' family home, but she had the top floor of the house to herself. It had been converted

107

into a spacious flat, and it was here that the party was held. Robyn was impressed by the large room, with its impressive, expensive-looking furnishings, where already about a dozen people stood chatting and sipping drinks. Fiona came forward to meet them, looking beautiful in a starkly simple black dress. Her blonde hair was twisted into a gleaming coronet and her only jewellery was a pair of sparkling earrings that looked expensive enough to be real diamonds.

Robyn was glad now that she hadn't bought the black dress, sure that next to Fiona she would have looked drab. Fay introduced her:

'Fiona, this is the friend I share Fell Cottage with – Robyn Seers.'

Fiona turned to Robyn with a smile. 'How do you do? I've heard so much about you.' She looked at Fay. 'When am I going to get an invitation to Fell Cottage, by the way? I keep waiting, but all in vain!'

'The trouble is that we're hardly ever off duty at the same time,' Fay told her. 'Tonight is a bit of a fluke.'

'Well, may I book the next fluke, please?' asked Fiona. 'If I don't invite myself I'll never get to see the place!' She took Robyn's arm. 'Come and be introduced to some people – I don't suppose you get much time for socialising in your job.'

Robyn could see what Fay had meant about Fiona being unspoilt. She had the sort of personality that seemed to draw people to her, warm and friendly; interested in others rather than herself, and Robyn had to admit that she was just the kind of girl Ross would admire, quite aside from the financial and social attributes she had to offer. In the corner of the room a buffet table was laden with good things. After introducing her to her other guests, Fiona led her to it.

'Do help yourself. In my experience people who work shifts never seem to eat properly.'

'It all looks delicious,' said Robyn, looking at the temptingly arranged delicacies. 'You must have been busy all day.'

'Well no, not really. I did it the lazy way and got a caterer,' Fiona admitted. She pursed her lips thoughtfully. 'Seers, Fay said your name was. Would that be with two E's?'

'That's right.' Robyn helped herself to some smoked salmon and an asparagus roll.

'It isn't a very common name, but I've a feeling I've come across it before.'

'Oh, I think there are quite a few of us

around…' Robyn stopped speaking as Fiona looked past her, her eyes suddenly lighting up.

'Ross! You managed to get here. How wonderful! Do come and meet Robyn Seers. She's a paramedic on the local ambulance team.'

'We've already met,' Ross said lightly, and Robyn felt her cheeks colouring.

Fiona smiled. 'You have? That's great. You can keep each other company for a minute while I go and circulate. One or two people are looking a little lost.' She was almost as tall as Ross and she put a hand on his shoulder as she passed, kissing him on the cheek before melting into the crowd.

Ross helped himself to a glass of wine from a tray on the table and stood looking at Robyn as though waiting for her to speak. She cleared her throat.

'She's very nice, Fiona.'

He nodded. 'I think so.'

'I'd gathered that.' She looked at the floor. 'I'm glad you're here…'

He looked surprised. 'You are?'

'Yes.' She moistened her dry lips. 'Because I owe you an apology – about yesterday. I didn't know about the hoax call until later.'

'I was on my way to young Ricky when the

emergency call came through,' he told her. 'I had to make a snap decision: which was the more urgent? Unfortunately I chose the wrong one.'

'But you could have been right.'

He shrugged. 'How good of you to give me the benefit of the doubt! Anyway, you were there, so no harm was done. You did a very good job, by the way. Congratulations.'

Robyn looked miserably into her glass, unable to assess just how much sincerity his words carried. 'Thanks. By the way, I wanted to speak to you – about what you said the other evening, at the cottage...'

She looked up and fond his eyes looking straight past her at Fiona on the other side of the room. She tried to read the expression in his eyes as he watched the tall, attractive girl laughing vivaciously with her guests. Was he thinking what a perfect doctor's wife she would make – an asset to a flourishing practice; the perfect hostess?

He spoke quietly, without taking his eyes off the other girl. 'This is a party, Robyn,' he reminded her. 'I think we should keep it light, don't you?'

Her colour rose. The look in his eyes stung her. 'Oh, don't worry, I wasn't planning to tell Fiona what happened,' she hissed at him. 'Unless you think a little healthy jealousy might strengthen your chances!'

Ross's eyes hardened as they returned to hers. He opened his mouth to say something, but at that moment Fiona rejoined them. Slipping an arm through Ross's, she said smilingly:

'There, now I can spend a little time with my favourite doctor.' She gave him a brilliant smile to which he responded, then, addressing herself to Robyn, she said:

'By the way, Robyn, I've heard all about you from young Danny Rawlings. Did you know he was off to the spinal unit at Ennermoor shortly?'

'No, I didn't. What's the latest news about him?'

Fiona shook her head. 'Poor boy, he's a very bad back injury, but there's still hope that he'll regain some use in his legs. If anyone can help, the Ennermoor team will. I'm sure he'd like to see you again before he goes.'

'I'll try to look in,' Robyn promised.

'I'll keep you posted about him if you like,' offered Fiona. 'I go over there sometimes to help out when their own physios have more work than they can handle.'

'Thanks. I'd like to know how he's getting

on.' Robyn looked around uneasily for an excuse to escape. She had the distinct impression that Ross would prefer her to make herself scarce so that he could talk to Fiona.

'Did you know him before his accident?' asked Fiona.

'Oh, no. It's just that his case interested me,' Robyn told her.

'For any particular reason?'

'No – I...' Robyn searched for words. 'I felt sorry for him, that's all. He's so young and – and...'

'I warned her about getting too involved with a patient,' Ross put in coolly. 'It can be disastrous. You shouldn't encourage her, Fiona.'

'I once knew another man who had the same kind of accident,' Robyn said defensively. 'One can't help being touched by a tragedy like that.' Looking up, she caught the surprised look on Ross's face. Fiona excused herself and went to greet more newcomers. Ross leaned towards her.

'You're full of surprises. Who was this mystery man?'

Robyn swallowed hard. 'Just – someone I wanted to help, but wasn't able to.'

He smiled cruelly. 'I see. *Did you walk out on him too?'*

'*Yes!* Yes, I did, as a matter of fact.' Tears stung her eyes and she turned, pushing her way unseeingly through the press of people until she reached a window that opened on to a balcony. The cool night air was like a balm to her burning cheeks and she stepped outside, leaning her back against the wall, wishing she could be anywhere but here. If only Bill would come, she would get him to take her home.

She closed her eyes, letting the tears slide down her cheeks as she thought of her brother, longing to see him and to have the chance of making up for the accident for which she still carried the guilt.

She didn't hear the quiet movement as Ross joined her on the balcony, and when she felt the handkerchief pressed into her hand her eyes flew open to stare at him.

'Here. This is getting to be a habit, isn't it?' He smiled ruefully. 'Look, I obviously said something that upset you. I'm sorry. Now, please come back to the party.'

She swallowed the tears, thrusting the handkerchief back at him. 'Don't worry. I'm not going to make things difficult for you.'

Ross sighed. 'You're a strange girl, Robyn. In spite of everything I don't understand you.'

'Who said you were supposed to?' she demanded. 'Who said I *wanted* you to? It would be easy if we could all be as simplistic as you. If all any of us wanted was a brilliant career and a lot of money; if we could all go through life *using* people to these ends!'

He laughed aloud. 'Is that what you think, Robyn? Is that how you really see me?'

She made to spin away from him and he caught at her waist as she stepped close to the low rail of the narrow balcony.

'Watch it!'

She gasped, half from shock at the glimpse she had had of the ground three fours below and half from the sudden impact of his hard body as he pulled her close against him. She felt his cheek brush hers. His lips were breathlessly close, but she stiffened, pushing her hands against his chest as she whispered:

'Let me go! You think all you have to do is to kiss me and I'll do anything you say. All that was over a long time ago, Ross.'

His arms slackened and he let her go. They stood staring at each other as she went on, adrenalin flowing fast, overriding the quickened beat of her heart:

'I won't spoil the party – make a scene, or whatever it is you're afraid of. You don't *matter* enough to me for that – understand?'

Stepping past him into the room, she took a deep breath. 'Round two to me!' she told herself. But as the beat of her heart gradually slowed to normal she knew it to be a hollow victory.

CHAPTER FIVE

Robyn escaped to the bedroom Fiona had set aside as a powder room, to check her make-up and to give herself a breathing space. When she returned to the party she found everyone dancing. To her relief no one seemed to have missed her. She stood for a moment in the doorway, watching the group of happy people enjoying themselves, and wished she too felt as carefree. On the far side of the room Ross was dancing with Fiona, laughing down at her as though he hadn't a care in the world. Stung, Robyn was about to turn away when suddenly hands covered her eyes from behind and she heard Bill's voice challenging:

'Guess who!'

'Bill!' She turned to him with a smile. 'You made it! I thought you might not.'

'Drove like a bat out of hell to be here as soon as I could,' he told her, taking her hand and leading her to mingle with the other dancers. A popular romantic song was being played and Bill pulled her close, resting his

117

cheek against hers.

'I hope you didn't drive dangerously,' she told him. 'It's stupid to take risks just for a party.'

'Who's bothered about a party?' he asked softly. 'Don't you know that I'd shoot rapids and fight tigers with my bare hands to be with you?'

Robyn laughed. 'Bill! It isn't worth driving like that. You are an idiot!'

'Barm-pot, I think is the local expression,' he corrected. 'And it *is* worth it. Please allow me to be the judge of that.'

The music stopped and she looked at him. 'I bet you haven't eaten either.'

'Well, no. Apart from a sandwich at the stadium, not since breakfast.'

She took his arm and led him towards the buffet table. 'In that case you'd better come and get something now. I'll introduce you to your hostess too, if I can see her.'

Bill stared at the lavish spread. 'Wow! Lavish, isn't it? Smoked salmon, no less, *and* if these old eyes don't deceive me, that's caviar over there! This beats curly cheese sandwiches any day!' He took a plate and began to help himself.

Robyn caught sight of Fiona and, taking Bill's arm, led him across the room to her.

'Fiona, this is Bill Hughes. He's a reporter on the local paper. Bill, this is Fiona, Dr Muir's daughter.'

As they were shaking hands Ross joined them. He looked at Bill with undisguised distaste.

'I read the touching story you did on the reconciliation of the Pearce couple,' he said sarcastically.

Bill smiled. 'I'm honoured!' He looked at Fiona. 'I doubt whether there's any job with quite as much opposition as mine,' he told her. 'If some people had their way news would never get reported at all.'

'Nor privacy invaded!' Ross continued to stare at Bill. 'Some of us have to uphold the right of the man in the street to a little dignity.'

Fiona, who had been looking from one to the other with a puzzled expression on her face, quickly jumped in:

'Well now, time everyone was dancing again. That tape seems to have run out. Ross, will you be a darling and change it for me?'

He turned reluctantly, with sceptical glance at Robyn. 'Of course.'

They returned to the buffet table where Bill enthusiastically refilled his plate. Robyn frowned at him. 'You needn't have come on quite so strong!'

He looked up from his plate, raising an eyebrow. 'Why not? He was the one who brought it up again. I don't have to take any old rubbish he likes to dish out!'

'It *is* a party,' she reminded him. 'Besides, he's Fiona's boy-friend.'

He stopped eating to stare at her. 'Ah! Do I detect a romance in the air? Are they engaged?'

'No! I don't know – I mean, I only assume…' Robyn grasped his wrist. 'Bill! You won't go and put *that* in the paper too, will you?'

He grinned. '*I* won't. I don't write the weekly gossip column, sweetheart, do I?'

Her fingers tightened convulsively round his wrist. 'Bill, you're here with me. The blame for anything you print about what you've heard here will fall on me. Just remember that, will you?'

'Stop worrying,' he told her. 'I shan't print anything. By the way, I have some news of another sort. You know we were speaking about taking a break so that I could show the Lake District off to you? Well, a friend of mine has this cottage at Windermere. He said I could have it any time now that the holiday season's over. We ought to go soon, before the weather breaks completely. Would you be free next weekend?'

Robyn was taken aback. She thought Bill had forgotten the idea of spending a weekend together. She didn't want to hurt him, but she didn't want to spend a weekend alone with him either, guessing that would only lead to more hurt. To give herself time to think, she reached for a sandwich.

'Do you think it's wise, Bill? It's almost winter now. The weather could be terrible.'

He grinned. 'Personally I can't think of anything more delightful than being marooned in a Lakeside cottage with you,' he said. 'Just think – no telephone, no television or radio, no neighbours. Just you and me – *bliss!*'

She was about to make a lighthearted rejoinder when she noticed Ross standing nearby. He was half turned away from them, but he was standing so close that he must clearly have heard what was being said. Instead of the remark she had been about to make, she said, on a sudden wicked impulse:

'It does sound tempting. Yes, Bill, I think it's a lovely idea. I should be free next weekend. You're right, it could be fun to take some time out.'

She had the satisfaction of seeing Ross's eyes swivel momentarily towards her. He *had* heard. Good! She was so triumphant that she completely failed to register the expression of surprised delight on Bill's face.

All thought of the Lakeside weekend had vanished from Robyn's mind when she received the call from Bill two days later. She was in the middle of a spell on night shift and was just getting up when the telephone rang. She answered it drowsily, looking at her watch. It was three-thirty in the afternoon.

'Hi there, sleepyhead. It's me,' a familiar voice greeted her.

Yawning, she pushed the hair back off her forehead. 'Oh, hello, Bill.'

'It's about our trip,' he told her. 'You haven't forgotten it's next weekend, have you? It's all arranged. I'm due for a long weekend.'

Her heart sank, as she remembered the enthusiasm she had displayed for Ross's benefit at the party. She had burned her boats now. There was no way out, it seemed.

'Oh–' She looked out of the window. Outside the sky was heavy with cloud, the sea a sheet of hammered lead. 'Are you really sure it's a good idea? The weather isn't particularly promising.'

'If I didn't know that you couldn't wait to be alone with me I'd think you'd gone off the idea,' he said. Then, in a less confident tone: 'You haven't, have you?'

Robyn sighed. In spite of his banter Bill was quite vulnerable at heart. She had promised, she supposed. It served her right for using him in order to get a jab in at Ross.

'No, of course I haven't,' she assured him. 'Though I do think the spring would be a better choice of seasons.'

The grey skies of the afternoon heralded a stormy night. By the time Robyn set out for Control a strong wind had sprung up, whipping the sea in the estuary into angry white-capped waves. As she went out to the car gusts of icy rain were flung in her face and she turned up her coat collar, hoping that she and Jim wouldn't be called out too often during the night.

Signing in, she took off her outdoor things and began, with Jim's help, to do the routine check of their vehicle and its extensive equipment. After that they put the kettle on for coffee and Jim looked across at her.

'Fancy a game of cards? Or do you want to look at the telly?'

Robyn didn't have time to reply, for at that moment the Station Officer opened the door.

'Okay, Ruby Two. Diabetic case – sounds as though it might be urgent. You know the drill with diabetics.' He gave Jim the details and they set off immediately.

Number twenty-three Jason's Close was a neat bungalow at the end of a short cul-de-sac, and as they drew up Robyn saw that all the lights seemed to be blazing. The front door was ajar and she pushed it open and went in. In the hall a large middle-aged lady was putting on a fur coat in front of the hall mirror. Robyn looked at her.

'Where's the patient?'

The woman smiled coyly. 'It's me.'

Jim, who stood behind Robyn, asked: 'You're a diabetic case, madam?'

'That's right.'

'And you have to be taken to hospital?'

The woman anchored a feathered hat with a vicious-looking pin. 'Not exactly, no.'

'Then where?' asked Robyn, glancing at Jim.

The woman turned to look at them. 'To the British Legion Hall, actually.'

The two looked at each other, then Jim cleared his throat. 'Look, madam, are you having us on? Is this some kind of joke?'

The woman looked shocked. 'Certainly not! I'm giving a lecture called "Coping With Diabetes" to the young wives' club and my car won't start. You wouldn't want me to let them down, would you? Not when it's something medical – and on a night like this! After all, I do pay my rates.'

Jim bit back a tart remark, not daring to look at Robyn. 'Well, I daresay we can drop you off there, just this once, as it's on our way back,' he said levelly. 'But please don't do this kind of thing again. Someone might genuinely need this ambulance. It isn't a taxi, you know.'

The woman, whose name turned out to be Mrs Robson, chattered all the way to the hall, and when she got out she tried in vain to give Jim a fifty-pence tip. As he put the vehicle in gear and pulled away from the kerb they looked at each other and burst out laughing simultaneously, giggling about the incident as Robyn completed the appropriate paperwork and radioed in to Control that they were available again.

'Go as quickly as possible to seventy-eight Wickham Road, Ruby Two. An acute appendicitis to go to the General. Doctor in attendance.'

Robyn replaced the microphone on its cradle and began to write out the slip. She looked at Jim, all traces of laughter now gone from her face.

'OK, Jim, all the stops out!'

A white-faced woman opened the door to them. 'Thank God! She's upstairs – her doctor's with her. We thought you were never coming!'

Jim handed Robyn the warmed blanket he carried and began to assemble the stretcher in the hall while she climbed the stairs. She had almost reached the top when a familiar voice addressed her in an urgent whisper:

'Hurry, please! The patient is three months' pregnant. We'll be lucky if she doesn't lose the child.'

Robyn began to explain the reason for their delay, but Ross took the blanket from her and turned away without waiting to hear what she had to say. She followed him into a bedroom where a young woman lay on the bed, her face white and drawn with pain. A young man in shirt sleeves, his hair dishevelled, sat holding her hand. Ross's grim expression changed to one of kindness as he bent over his patient.

'The ambulance is here now,' he told her quietly. 'We'll have you tucked up in hospital in no time at all.' He patted her shoulder. 'Try not to worry – we'll soon have you well again.'

He was rewarded by a smile from the girl, but her young husband stood up and, turning aside, asked quietly:

'She won't lose the baby, will she, Doctor? She wants it so badly.'

Ross's face was grave as he looked into the young man's eyes.

'She's a strong girl. We'll do our best, I promise you that.' He glanced at Robyn meaningly. 'Speed is of the essence in cases like this. Every minute counts!'

She knew it was a reproof and longed to explain, but there was no time. She and Jim wrapped the girl warmly and carried her gently down the stairs to the waiting stretcher. Once in the ambulance Jim made as much speed as he could, driving with the utmost care to avoid any unnecessary jolting. At the General the Sister from A & E and two porters were waiting and the patient was quickly transferred to a trolley and whisked off to the theatre, leaving her husband looking lost and forlorn as he began his long vigil. Robyn looked at him helplessly, then at Jim.

'Damn that selfish woman and her lecture!'

she said vehemently. 'If only people realised how vital even a few minutes can be.'

Jim nodded his agreement. 'It's amazing what some people think paying their rates entitles them to! They never learn, though – until it's *their* turn to be ill.'

As they left the hospital Robyn looked round, hoping she might get a glimpse of Ross, but he was nowhere to be seen. Reluctantly, she followed Jim out to their waiting vehicle where already the radio was crackling demandingly. She sighed. It was going to be a busy night.

Robyn was ready when Bill called for her on Friday afternoon. Even though there was little improvement in the weather she looked forward to a break. She hardly remembered such a busy spell on nights as the one she had just completed. As they drove eastwards towards Windermere, she told Bill about it.

'One thing, you can't complain that your job is boring,' he observed. 'All that drama!' He glanced round at her, smiling. 'You really care about them all, don't you? I mean, it's not just a job to you.'

'It doesn't do to feel things too much, but I don't think I could do it if I didn't care.' She looked thoughtful for a moment. 'I have to admit that it does play havoc with the nerves at times. That's why it's nice to get away.'

'I hope that isn't the only reason' he said wryly.

As the car climbed higher the scenery became more and more spectacular. Robyn had never been to Norway, but she imagined it would be just like this; distant mountains, some with the first winter snow crowning their peaks; clustered pines and clean, sparkling air. They descended the steep road to the Lakeside town with its busy hotels, shops and boat-hire firms. Robyn was surprised to see that there were still quite a few tourists about in spite of the lateness of the season. Bill looked at her.

'Would you like to stop here for tea before we go on to the cottage?'

'Oh, yes, please,' Robyn said eagerly.

The outdoor tables at the Princess Restaurant with their gay umbrellas had been taken inside for the season, but they sat at a table in the window overlooking the Lake and ate hot buttered toast and cream cakes. Robyn was enchanted. Even the cloudy sky couldn't take away the beauty of the scene spread before her. The mantle of snow and purple mist worn by the distant hills made her shiver with awe.

'It's so vast!' she said, gazing out across the sheet of water. 'I can't even see the other shore. And so dramatic and beautiful.'

'There are less commercialised lakes,' Bill said cynically. 'But beggars can't be choosers. This was where the cottage was, so here it had to be.'

'It's lovely. Where is the cottage, by the way?'

'More a cabin than a cottage, actually, and quite a way from the town, thank goodness,' Bill told her. 'I wouldn't call it a quiet weekend, staying down here – all those madly energetic types boating, water-skiing and windsurfing. So *frenetic!* No, you wait till you see our little hidey-hole. I think you'll be pleased.'

She was! Driving to the far side of the lake, Bill parked the car, then led her down to where two small wood-built cabins nestled among trees. A little further down the trees opened out on to a tiny 'beach' with a small landing stage where a boat was moored. Robyn took a deep breath of the pine-scented air and stretched her arms luxuriously, looking out across the gently rippling water.

'Oh, it must be heaven here in the summer. Does the boat belong to the cottage too?'

'Afraid not,' Bill told her. He pointed to the other cottage, almost hidden by shrubs and trees, about a hundred yards away. 'See that place? Some wealthy couple bought it and did it up with every imaginable luxury. They come down for weekends or let it to their posh friends. The boat belongs to them.'

'Do you think they're there this weekend?' asked Robyn, peering through the trees.

Bill shrugged. 'Couldn't say.' He rubbed his hands. 'Now, what about some supper? I'm starving!'

He took her on a tour of the little cabin, which had been specially built for holidays and weekends. The living quarters were open-plan; a large living-room-cum-kitchen, divided by a breakfast bar. Robyn was slightly dismayed to find that there was only one bedroom. Reading her thoughts, Bill said:

'You can have this, of course. I'll doss down on the couch in there.'

Back in the kitchen Robyn unpacked the box of food Bill had brought with him and began to make a meal. He had included a supply of frozen food, so it didn't take long. As she worked Bill was busy unpacking his bag, throwing his things on to the couch in the living-room.

'You've brought your camera,' she observed, watching him from the kitchen. 'Are you expecting to take photographs?'

He spun round, looking slightly guilty. 'Oh– Well, you never know what might crop up,' he said. 'I'd kick myself if I happened on a good story and wasn't prepared for it, wouldn't I?'

She looked at him thoughtfully for a moment. Bill was a dedicated and ambitious reporter. Could all that enthusiasm he had displayed over spending this weekend with her have been some sort of cover-up? It would be one explanation for the doubtful choice of timing. She smiled wryly to herself as she turned the fish fingers in the frying pan. If that were the case it really would serve her right. Her own reasons for coming were equally devious, after all.

By the time they had eaten it was dusk. Bill helped with the washing-up, then suggested a walk down to the lake before darkness fell. It was chilly, a fresh wind whipping the surface of the lake into miniature waves. Robyn huddled into her anorak and as they stood watching the lights of the town twinkling on the opposite shore Bill slipped an arm round her shoulders.

'Enjoying yourself?' he asked, smiling down at her.

She glanced up at him. 'Yes. It's lovely.' She hesitated. 'Bill, don't be cross, but you have another reason for being here this weekend, haven't you?'

He hunched his shoulders, not meeting her eyes. 'Why should you think that?'

She shrugged. 'Just something you said – and the fact that you brought your camera.'

For a moment he looked as though he would protest, then he gave up with a laugh. 'Nothing much misses you, does it? OK, I suppose I'd better come clean. It's that other cottage. I had it from a reliable source that a certain pop star would be there this weekend, entertaining a lady he doesn't want the public to know about.'

'Bill!' Robyn was shocked. 'There's a name for what you're planning, you know. How would you like it? Besides, is that the kind of thing the *Courier* will be interested in?'

He laughed. 'You're joking! Who's talking about the *Courier?* If I get an exclusive on this, one of the nationals will pay well for it – specially with a photograph. Then there are the pop mags. This kind of thing is just what the fans love. I might even try the telly!'

'But surely everyone has a right to some privacy,' she protested.

He shook his head. 'Not when you're a pop star, love. When you go in for that kind of life you sell your soul to the media.'

She was thoughtful as they walked back to the cottage. 'I wish you'd mentioned this before,' she said uneasily. 'I'd really rather not be involved in this kind of thing. Why didn't you tell me?'

He grinned down at her wryly. 'I think you've just answered that one yourself. Besides, I *did* want to spend some time with you too, you know that's true.'

'Kill two birds with one stone, you mean?'

'Oh, Robbie, that's unkind!'

As they stood looking at each other in the tiny kitchen Bill put his hands on her shoulders and drew her towards him. 'Look, there's a bottle of wine in the fridge. How about making some sandwiches to go with it? I'm going to slip out for half an hour. When I get back we'll have a nice cosy evening and the rest of the weekend will be ours alone. What do you say?'

'What are you going to do?' She narrowed her eyes suspiciously.

'Ask no questions, hear no lies.' He wagged a finger at her. 'You said you didn't want to be involved. Well, you needn't if you follow that simple rule.' He shrugged into his leather jacket and zipped it up firmly, bending to kiss her cheek. 'Back soon, sweetheart.'

Robyn pretended not to notice the expensive camera with its telescopic lens that he had hidden under the jacket when he thought she wasn't looking.

It was about fifteen minutes later that she heard the noise – angry shouting, followed by a blood-curdling yell, then silence. Heart thudding with apprehension, she opened the cabin door a few inches and peered out into the darkness. It was like black velvet outside; the kind of darkness peculiar to deep, wooded countryside. Robyn shivered.

'Bill!' she called anxiously. 'Bill, are you there?' At first there was nothing, and she was about to turn away when a twig snapped close by and she heard someone breathing heavily.

'Who is it? Who's there?' Seized by a sudden panic, she had turned and begun to push the door shut when a hand shot out and grabbed her wrist. She opened her mouth to scream, then Bill stepped into the slice of light coming from the open door.

'For God's sake don't lock me out! That's

all I need!'

She stared at him aghast. The leather of his jacket was ripped and streaked with dirt and the blood that was pouring from his nose. 'Bill! What on earth...' She reached out to help him inside.

In the kitchen she fetched water and towels and began to clean him up, fetching ice from the fridge to stop the bleeding. As she folded the cubes inside a cloth and laid them across the bridge of his nose he let out an anguished yell. Both eyes were rapidly closing to swollen, discoloured slits and she strongly suspected that his nose was broken. 'Bill, can you tell me what happened?' she asked him gently.

'That bastard hit me,' he told her painfully from between clenched teeth. 'Sneaked up behind me and before I knew it – *Ouch!*' He winced as she examined his swollen nose with expert fingers.

'Look, I think I ought to get you to a hospital, and maybe we should report this to the police,' she told him seriously. 'It looks to me as though you have a case for assault.'

'*No!*' Bill leapt up, then winced and put a hand up to his face again. 'No, I'm not having the fuzz in on it. I'd rather this was kept between you and me.' He peered up at her pathetically with bloodshot eyes. 'I suppose it's what you might call an occupational hazard. Only the editor of the *Courier* might not quite see it that way. He's not exactly noted for his understanding nature.'

Robyn opened her mouth to ask him just what he had done to invite the attack, then thought better of it. Perhaps the less she knew, the better.

'Where's your camera?' she asked as she helped him out of the ruined jacket.

He sighed resignedly. 'Somewhere out there.' He jerked a thumb over his shoulder. 'About twelve fathoms deep into Lake Windermere, I shouldn't wonder.'

'Oh, Bill!' She looked down at him. 'Your expensive camera!'

'It's not the camera I'm worried about, it's what was *in* it,' he told her bitterly. 'I'd have made a fortune with what was on that film.'

She fetched a thick sweater from his bag and helped him into it, ignoring his protestations that he would be fine in the morning.

'We're going to find you a doctor,' she told him firmly. 'I don't want to worry you, but I'd be happier if you had that little lot X-rayed. Come on, we'll stop at the first pub

137

we come to and ask the way to the nearest hospital.'

The first pub was on about a mile down the road. Robyn drew the car onto the forecourt and peered up at the swinging sign that creaked in the freshening wind: The Fox and Grapes.

'You'd better stay here,' she told Bill. 'I'll go in and ask the landlord where we can find a doctor or a hospital, whichever is nearest.' As she went to get out of the car she suddenly thought of something and turned to him. 'What do you want to say you did?' she asked. 'We'd better both have the same story.'

He shrugged miserably. 'Say a mountain fell on me. That's what it feels like!'

As she opened the door of the bar warm air rushed out to meet her. It was crowded with locals and late holidaymakers, all relaxing after the week's work, and she had to struggle to get to the bar. At last she faced the landlord, a stout, red-faced man with a jovial smile.

'I wonder, could you tell me if there's a hospital near here – or a doctor?' she asked. 'I've got my friend outside in the car. He's had rather a nasty accident, and I think his nose is broken.'

The man looked concerned. 'Dear, dear, sorry to hear that.' He stroked his chin thoughtfully. 'Hospital's quite a way from here. Tell you what…' He reached for a large bell that stood on the bar and rang it. In the ensuing hush he called out: 'Is there a doctor in the house? Young lady here says there's been an accident.'

Robyn looked around at the sea of faces as all eyes trained upon her in the ensuing silence. There was a subdued murmur as they consulted with each other, then a voice from somewhere at the back said, loudly and clearly:

'Yes, I'm a doctor.'

All eyes swivelled to the owner of the voice who was elbowing his way through the mass of drinkers. As they parted to let him through and Robyn saw him her heart sank. Of all people, it was Ross St Clair!

CHAPTER SIX

'If you'll take me to the patient I'll see what I can do. Was he involved in a car accident?'

Ross's face was expressionless. He showed no surprise at seeing Robyn; indeed, an onlooker would not even have known that they were acquainted.

'Not exactly.' Robyn led the way out of the bar. In the comparative quiet of the lobby she turned to him.

'It's Bill Hughes,' she told him. His expression remained impassive.

'I thought it might be.'

'He – he had an accident, a blow to the face. I think his nose is broken, but there doesn't seem to be any concussion.' He seemed to be waiting for further information and she added, 'He – er – fell.' She opened the door. 'He's just out there. In the car– Oh!' As she turned someone came through the door to join them. It was Fiona Muir, dressed in immaculate country tweeds. 'Oh, hello.'

'Hello, Robyn. I came to see if there was

anything I could do. I hope your friend isn't seriously hurt.'

'I suggest we go and see.' Grim-faced, Ross went ahead of them through the door, Robyn following, wondering what Bill would say when he saw who was about to minister to him.

With the aid of a torch and the interior light of the car Ross examined Bill's face while the two girls stood anxiously waiting. At last he straightened up and turned to Robyn.

'You were right, his nose is broken. Looks nasty.' He looked at Bill. 'How did you say you did it?'

'Walked into a lamp-post,' Bill muttered.

Ross looked from one to the other, his eyebrows rising momentarily, then he said decisively: 'Mmm – well, I'd like it X-rayed. I think we should get you to the nearest hospital.'

There was a strangled protest from Bill. 'No! I want to get back to Crownhaven,' he insisted. 'I have to be at work on Monday morning whatever happens. I can't be stuck out here in the sticks!'

Ross looked at Robyn. 'Can you drive him back? I'll get my bag and give him an injection for the pain. I daresay they'll discharge him tomorrow if there's no concussion.'

Fiona was peering into the back of the little car with its jumble of equipment.

'Surely poor Bill would be more comfortable in your car, Ross,' she suggested. 'We were going home anyway. He could stretch out in the back. Robyn can follow us in this one, can't you?'

Robyn was acutely embarrassed. 'Oh, but it would spoil your evening. I don't want to…'

'Not at all. It's a good idea.' Ross helped a still protesting Bill out of the car and into his own, which was parked on the other side of the car park. A moment later Robyn was watching helplessly as the sleek black car pulled on to the road and slid smoothly away. She could just make out Bill's swollen face gazing despondently out of the rear window at her.

She drove thoughtfully back to the cottage, collected their belongings and packed them into the car, then, locking up securely, she set off on the road to Crownhaven. Poor Bill, his plans for a romantic *and* profitable weekend had come to a sad end.

At the hospital she parked Bill's car and went into the Accident and Emergency department. The Sister on duty was a friend of Fay's and recognised her at once.

'Hello. Can't keep away from the place even when you're off duty, eh?'

'Has a Mr Bill Hughes arrived with Dr St Clair?' Robyn asked.

'Yes,' Sister nodded. 'Nasty facial injury. Duty houseman admitted him and he's gone up to X-Ray.'

'I've brought his car.' Robyn handed her the keys. 'Perhaps you could give him these.'

'Of course. I daresay he'll be allowed home tomorrow if there are no complications.'

Ignoring the woman's enquiring glance, Robyn was just turning away when she caught sight of Ross coming down the stairs. She turned quickly, but she was too late; he had seen her. Reluctantly, she waited by the door.

She glanced at him as he caught her up. 'How is he?'

'He'll live,' he said briefly. 'Better to stay in overnight and have a check-up, though.' He looked at her speculatively. 'A pity. It must have ruined your weekend.'

'Yours too. I'm sorry. Where is Fiona, by the way?'

'Gone home. And we were only out for the day,' he corrected.

They were outside in the car park now and

he looked round. 'How are you getting back to Ravenshore?'

'Oh!' Robyn remembered that she now had no means of transport. 'I shall manage.'

He took her arm. 'You'd better let me take you. But first I think you'd better come back with me for a nightcap. You look all in.'

She opened her mouth to protest, but he was hurrying her along so fast that she hadn't the breath.

His car was comfortable and smelt luxuriously of new leather. In the passenger seat she clipped on her safety belt and tried hard not to think as he started the whisper-quiet engine and drove out of the hospital car park on to the road.

Ross glanced at her quizzically. 'Going to tell me what really happened?'

She bit her lip. 'I already have.'

'Yes, and so did he – the two accounts didn't quite tally, did they? Which is the true version? You can tell me. You know I won't betray a confidence.'

'It's not *my* confidence to betray,' she told him.

'Isn't it?' He glanced at her with a grin. 'I was rather hoping it was. I'll confess I was rather hoping *you'd* done it.'

'*Me?*' She stared at him. 'Hit Bill on the

nose? You're not serious?'

He chuckled. 'Couldn't be more so. If ever a nose cried out to be punched it's his!' He gave her a wry grin. 'And I seem to remember you can pack quite a wallop when roused!'

Robyn felt her cheeks burn. 'You have a convenient memory,' she told him dryly. 'Anyway, no one has ever roused me in the same way that you did.'

'I'm flattered to hear it!'

Even in the dimness of the car she could see his eyes twinkling and she winced at her choice of words.

'You know what I mean,' she muttered under her breath.

'I know that you seem to have lost your sense of humour since we last met,' he said. 'And that's a pity – it used to be one of your better attributes. Now, are you going to tell me what happened to Hughes?'

'He – had a sort of – argument with someone,' she said slowly.

'I see. Care to elucidate further?' He glanced at her.

'He was on the track of a story, and the subject of it chose violence as a means of showing his displeasure.'

'Oh, *very* nicely put,' Ross said cynically.

146

'In other words, he was snooping as usual and someone gave him his come-uppance. Well, he had it coming.'

'Bill would be the first to agree,' she told him. 'It's part of his job. An occupational hazard, he called it. I wanted to report the matter to the police, but he wouldn't let me.'

'I'm glad to hear he has *some* sense. He probably knew he'd get the worst end of it if he had! The law doesn't take kindly to snoopers.'

Robyn swallowed her desire to tell him not to be so pompous. She was relying on him for a lift home, after all.

The car drew on to the forecourt of an exclusive-looking block of flats. Ross switched off the ignition and released his seat belt. Getting out, he came round to open the door for her.

'Come up and have a coffee. You look as though you could do with it.'

She hesitated, torn between a desire to see the inside of the place where he lived and a wish to escape from his probing mood.

'Well, if you're not coming you'll have to wait in the car for me,' he told her. 'The last bus will have gone and I'm not driving all that way without a hot drink.'

As there seemed to be no argument, she got out and followed him to the lift. He was silent as they sped silently upwards. His flat was on the top floor and as he opened the door she caught the same scent of newness she had encountered in the car. When he switched on the lights she saw that no expense had been spared. Thick cream-coloured carpet covered the floors and the lounge he showed her into was furnished with comfortable, stylish furniture. Twin settees upholstered in dark green velvet flanked a fireplace made of creamy-coloured marble veined with green. Between them stood an onyx-topped coffee table. A shallow dais led to a wide picture window reaching almost from floor to ceiling and giving a breathtaking view. Robyn could see the town spread below like a glittering display of jewels on black velvet. In the distance she could see the ships anchored in the dock, their masts tipped with lights reflected in the water. Ross saw her looking at it.

'It's a nice view. Distance always lends a certain enchantment, doesn't it? But I think we'll shut it out for the present.' He crossed the room and pulled the cord that swung the long green velvet curtains across the window, hiding the splendour from view. He switched on a large cream-shaded table lamp that gave the room a soft, warm glow.

'There, that's better. Now…' he looked at her enquiringly as he opened a glass-fronted cabinet full of bottles, 'I suggest a stiff bandy.'

'I thought you said coffee.'

'We can have coffee later.' He poured a generous measure of brandy and handed her the balloon-shaped glass. 'For heaven's sake relax, Robbie. I'm not going to eat you,' he said with sudden impatience. 'Perhaps some music will help.'

He went across to a music centre enclosed in a wall unit that also housed books. She saw that he still had his collection of detective novels, then she noticed something else – the Bacarat glass paperweight in the shape of a rabbit that she had bought him when he had gained his fellowship. So he had kept it. Somehow, the sight of it sitting there among the familiar books brought a lump to her throat as memories flooded back. Although this room was totally new, totally strange to her, the essence of all they had shared was still here. Perhaps it always would be wherever Ross was, she told herself despairingly.

She took a sip of her brandy and choked a

little as the fiery liquid seared her throat.

'There.' He turned to her with a smile as the first strains of Mendelssohn's Italian Symphony filled the room. 'Do you remember this? The week we spent in Italy – that day at San Marino, sipping Moscata at the top of the highest of the three peaks with this music in our ears?' He laughed. 'I never knew whether it was the height, the wine, or the music that made you so dizzy.'

'It was the height. You know I never could stand heights. I get dizzy standing on a chair.' Robyn's voice was light, but the memory brought a stab of pain to her heart. How could she ever forget that holiday? It was the only one they had ever spent together and all the more memorable because it had been spontaneous. They had both found themselves suddenly free and had flown out on impulse. But remembering could only hurt, so why remind her?

'Can we go now?' She put her half-finished drink down on the coffee table, but when she straightened up again she found Ross standing close to her.

'What's the matter, Robyn, don't you like my flat?' he asked her.

She turned so that he couldn't see her face. Was he aware of how taunting his words sounded? Did he know that seeing this flat she was sharply and painfully reminded of another; of the one they had shared? It hadn't been nearly as large and grand as this, but it too had been near a river. In the daytime the view was of drab rooftops and bustling humanity; of grey polluted water flowing sluggishly by. But at night it was magically transformed, just as this one was, into jewelled magnificence, remote and romantic.

'I think your flat is very nice,' she told him inadequately. 'It's just that I have no place in it.'

He sighed and crossed the room to her. Taking her hand, he pressed the half-full glass of brandy back into it. 'We'll go when I'm ready, Robyn.' His voice was firm yet gentle. 'I want to talk to you – talk without all these barriers you keep putting up. Now, please, drink your brandy – sit down.'

She felt trapped. There was nothing she could do but obey him. Unfortunately she could not get home without his help. She swallowed the brandy in her glass at one gulp and made no protest when he refilled it.

'All right, let's get it over,' she challenged as she took a seat on the settee. 'What do you want to talk about?'

'About you.' He sat down opposite her.

She shrugged. 'What about me? I'm the same unremarkable person I was two years ago.'

'And who *is* that?' he demanded. 'I'm beginning to think I never knew you, Robyn, even then. I never fully understood why you walked out after agreeing to marry me. One minute you seemed thrilled at the prospect – the next, furious and indignant; complaining about being expected to give everything up for the mere state of marriage.' He held up his hand. 'But I don't want to re-open old quarrels again. It was your choice to call it a day and I respect that. What I can't forgive is that you were obviously playing a part all the time we were together. The girl I loved wasn't the real Robyn at all!'

The past tense of 'loved' didn't escape her, and there was a sharp edge to her voice as she asked: 'What can any of it possibly matter now?'

Ross shrugged. 'Perhaps you're right.'

She smiled. The brandy was relaxing her, blurring the edges of the hurt and making everything seem suddenly crystal clear. 'You needn't think you're fooling me, you know,

Ross. What you really can't forgive is the wound your gigantic ego suffered, and you'd like to find some flaw in my character to soothe it for you. Really, Ross, what do you take me for? Why don't you just take me home and forget the whole unhappy episode?'

'Then there's this man in your past.' He went on as though she hadn't spoken. 'The one you spoke of the other night at Fiona's party. You never mentioned him before.'

'And I'm not going to now!' Robyn told him firmly, getting to her feet. 'I might as well ask you to explain your relationship with Fiona, and I wouldn't *dream* of doing that. So, as our conversation seems to have come to an end, will you please take me home? If you want to know, I think it's despic – despic...' She frowned at her sudden inability to form the word. Ross took the glass from her hand and gently eased her back on to the settee.

'When did you last eat?' he asked.

She blinked as the dizziness passed. 'I had a perfectly substant – sub – a good meal at supper time.'

He laughed. 'Oh, Robyn, I'm sorry. I forgot – you never could drink, could you? Remember that party we gave after you passed your paramedic exams?'

'I don't remember anything about it,' she told him indignantly.

'I'm not surprised!' He laughed, dropping down beside her on the settee. She knew she should get up now, go to the bathroom and splash her face with cold water, but the settee felt so soft, so warm and comfortable. She did stiffen a little when Ross's arm slid round her shoulders, but the weight of it prevented her from getting up.

'It was a shock, seeing you that day,' she told him softly. 'Knowing that you'd come to work in Crownhaven.'

'For me too. Why did you choose to come here?'

She shrugged. 'It was as far away from everything I wanted to forget as possible,' she told him.

'But why was it so important to forget, Robyn?' he insisted. 'Splitting up was *your* choice.'

She twisted round to look at him. 'Now who's playing a part? When I marry it will be to a man who wants me for myself. Not because I happen to fit into his plans at that particular moment. I want a man who wants me beside him for better reasons than – than...' She shook her head. It was all coming out wrong. It sounded so *stupid,* like something from an agony column. Not only that, but she was aware that he was laughing at her. She could feel him shaking. Turning, she glared at him.

'You see, to you it's all a big *joke!*'

'It isn't. I promise you it isn't.' He tried hard, but the corners of his mouth twitched.

'Then why are you laughing?'

'Because you're so funny when you're slightly squiffy.'

'I am *not* squiffy, but if I were it'd be your fault!' Furious, she tried to struggle to her feet, but the arm that lay across her shoulders tightened. His other hand cupped her chin, turning her face towards him, and she found herself looking straight into his eyes. She tried to analyze the look in them. It was soft and amused – but more than that.

'Oh, Robbie, where are you? Come out from behind that reinforced concrete for a minute, will you?' he asked softly.

She couldn't speak. Her eyes locked with his as though mesmerised. It was like waking from a dream, a bad dream. All the resistance drained out of her body, and when Ross's mouth came down on hers she had the curious sensation that she was melting.

Her arms crept round his neck, her fingers twining into the thick copper hair, while her lips parted yieldingly under his. She heard herself whisper his name as his lips paused at the corner of her mouth, then brushed across her cheek. As her head fell back she shivered at the ecstasy of his mouth on her throat. Then he was unzipping her anorak, pressing his lips warmly into the hollow of her throat. When he slid the anorak over her shoulders and down her arms, she moved co-operatively, and when he began, very slowly, to unbutton her shirt she blotted out the shrill warning that rang in her head, tingling from head to foot at the sheer delight that was in his touch.

Weak with longing, she closed her ears to the persistent inner voice that told her he didn't love her. She had wanted to be in his arms like this ever since the day she had looked up and found herself face to face with him again. She hadn't the strength to deny it any longer. He might not love her any more, but at least at this moment he wanted her – maybe almost as much as she wanted him.

She felt the strong beat of his heart vibrating through her as he pulled her closer, the hardness of his body pressing demandingly against hers. Opening her eyes, she read the smouldering question in his eyes and in reply she sought his lips again, wrapping her arms tightly round him. Her whole being cried out her love for him, but she never knew whether she spoke or not, caught up in the dizzy, intoxicating wonder that was Ross's lovemaking.

She was not aware of falling asleep or of how long she slept but at first when she woke she thought she had dreamed the whole thing. Reluctant to wake properly, she lay there, stretching sensuously as she recalled the dream in delicious detail, until she opened her eyes and saw that she still lay on the settee among the scattered cushions. Someone – presumably Ross – had tucked a blanket round her. She sighed. It was so warm and comfortable here. If only she didn't have to awake fully and face the complications that were reality!

'You're awake, then?'

She opened her eyes and looked up to see him standing over her, a steaming cup in his hands.

'Here, I've made you a cup of tea. I take it it's still your first priority when you wake up.'

She struggled into a sitting position, holding the blanket against her as she became suddenly aware of her nakedness. 'What time is it?'

'Seven o'clock.'

She gasped. 'Fay will wonder what happened to me!'

Ross smiled. 'Fay thinks you're away for the weekend, doesn't she?'

She relaxed. 'Oh yes.' She sipped the tea gratefully. 'All the same, I suppose I should go home.'

He sat down on the edge of the settee. 'I don't see why.' He looked very handsome this morning, wearing a casual polo-neck sweater and slacks. He smelled of soap and after-shave, and Robyn was seized with the desire to feel his smooth skin under her lips again. Blushing, she looked away, unable to meet his eyes. Somehow, in the cold light of day she felt shy and embarrassed with him. Burying her face in the teacup, she said nothing.

'I've got to go out for a while. I'm on Sunday call and there's a patient I have to look in on,' he told her. 'Why don't you get dressed while I'm gone. We could spend the day together even if we can't go out.'

She chewed her lip doubtfully. 'I should really go and see how Bill is.'

158

He pulled a wry face. 'All right, I don't mind, as long as you come straight back here.'

She looked at him. 'Is that what you really want? I mean, you don't have to – because of last night...' She trailed off as he took her chin in his hand and made her look at him.

'Robbie! We really have to talk. You must see that now?'

She nodded and he stood up. 'I'll be back as soon as I can. Have a nice long bath. I think you'll approve of the bathroom, by the way. Maybe when I get back we can have breakfast.'

When he had gone Robyn got up and, wrapping the blanket around herself sarong fashion, went in search of the bathroom. When she opened the door she gasped. Ross had been right – she *did* approve. It really was gorgeous. The deep pile of the pale green carpet was soft under her bare toes as she turned on the taps and watched the water gush into the ivory-coloured sunken bath out of golden dolphin-shaped taps. The wall opposite was entirely covered in mirror, while a marble-topped vanity unit with twin basins took up another. Looking for towels, she found that the mirrors slid back to reveal a spacious, heated linen cupboard. On the wide windowsill a veritable jungle of tropical plants flourished, cool and green against the ivory and gold tiles.

A long soak in the bath refreshed her, but as she climbed into the shirt and jeans she had worn last night she couldn't help wishing she had something more glamorous to wear. She combed her hair into a halo of damp curls and left it to dry naturally, then, after applying a dash of lipstick, she went into the kitchen to start breakfast.

The telephone was on the kitchen wall and beside it, on the shelf, an answering machine. She switched it on, in case there had been any calls for Ross while she was in the bath. There was a short call from Dr Muir, asking Ross to look in on an elderly patient early this morning. That would be where he was now. She was just about to switch it off when there was a click and another voice began to speak:

'Ross. It's me, Fiona. I expect you're out on a call, but I'll say what I have to say anyhow, before I lose my nerve and chicken out. As a matter of fact it's easier this way. I think I'd have been too embarrassed to say this while you were actually there – on the other end of the line.'

Robyn's hand hovered over the switch.

This was quite clearly going to be private, but as the voice went on she knew she had to hear it out.

'Ross, I've been thinking over what we've talked about today and I know you're right. It *is* what I want really. I think you already knew that. It was your reason for taking me out for that long walk today, wasn't it?' She laughed. 'It's quite uncanny at times, the way you seem to understand me. Ever since we first met, out in Saudi, you've been so sweet and understanding. As you know, I've never felt ready to settle for marriage before, but now I know it's what I want. I'd like to say my career held me back till now, but I know it wouldn't be any use trying to pull the wool over your eyes. You understand me far too well for that. So the answer's going to be yes, darling, for better, for worse, as they say. Ring me when you can and we'll arrange a celebration. Oh, and Ross – thanks again for a lovely day – and for the offer.'

Robyn stood staring at the machine long after it was silent. Ross must have switched off before he got to this call. What did it mean? Deep in her heart she knew there was only one answer. Ross had taken Fiona out yesterday and asked her to marry him. She

161

had asked for time to think about it – and this was her answer. What had happened between them last night had been an impulsive thing; born out of habit, or worse, Ross trying to show her that he could still twist her round his little finger. Trying with considerable success too, she told herself bitterly. This morning – especially when he heard Fiona's message – he might have cause to regret it. Well, she could save them both the awkwardness of that. She could leave right now!

Swiftly, she gathered her few things together and scribbled a note which she left propped up against the Bacarat paper-weight:

'Ross, I thought it better to leave. Sorry about last night. It shouldn't have happened. I'm sure you don't need any more complications in your life. Good luck. Robyn.'

CHAPTER SEVEN

The buses to Ravenshore were few and far between, and Robyn found she had two hours to lose, so she decided to go to the hospital and visit Danny Rawlings. He would be off to the spinal unit any day now. She could look in on Bill too if he was still there.

Inside, her heart was like lead. If only she could turn back the clock! She would have given anything to erase the previous night. If only Ross had taken Fiona somewhere else for the day yesterday; if only they could have chosen some place other than the Fox and Grapes to have a drink before starting for home. Sometimes fate seemed especially spiteful.

She was on her way up the stairs when she looked up and saw Bill coming towards her. She was glad to see that he looked much better. The swelling had gone down quite a bit since last night, but his eyes were still puffy and badly discoloured. Nevertheless he looked pleased to see her.

'Robbie! It's good to see you. Don't tell me you've come all the way out from Ravenshore just to see me?'

She shrugged noncommittally. It was impossible to explain the truth about how she came to be here. 'How's the nose?' she asked him. 'Still hurt?'

'Only when I laugh,' he told her wryly. 'Not a serious fracture, apparently, though. Should heal without spoiling my beauty too much, so at least that's something.' He fingered the injured nose tenderly.

'I dare say it'll be a long time before you tangle with incognito pop stars again,' Robyn suggested as they walked.

He gave her a puffy, lopsided grin. 'I wouldn't bet on that if I were you.'

'I was going to look in on Danny Rawlings too, if Sister will let me,' she told him. 'He'll be moving on soon and I'd like to say goodbye.'

'Great. I'll come with you.' He took her arm and they began to walk along the corridor towards Men's Surgical. Bill held up the bag he carried.

'Apparently St Clair looked in earlier and left my bag,' he told her. 'That's why I'd given up hope of seeing you.'

'Oh– Sorry, I'd forgotten your bag. It was

164

all so fraught last night,' Robyn said un-happily.

He looked at her with concern. 'I know – I'm sorry. Are you all right, Robbie? You look a bit under the weather.'

'Thanks for the compliment. I'm fine,' she told him. She hoped he wasn't going to enquire how she got to the hospital this morning and why she hadn't used her own car, but it seemed he had other things on his mind.

'I wouldn't blame you if you never spoke to me again after what happened,' he said morosely. 'To tell the truth, when they told me St Clair had dropped my bag off I thought that was it – that it was all over between us.'

'Oh, don't be so silly, Bill,' she said abruptly.

The Sister on Men's Surgical agreed to let them in to see Danny for a few minutes and they found him quite cheerful and clearly looking forward to moving on to the spinal unit. But as they chatted together, Robyn could see there was something on his mind. She guessed he wouldn't tell her what it was in front of a stranger, so after a while she suggested that Bill slipped down to the cafeteria to get some magazines and chocolate. He agreed at once, and when he had gone she turned to the boy in the bed.

'Is there something on your mind, Danny?' she asked.

He hesitated for a moment, his face clouded, then he said: 'It's Mum.'

'Your mother? She's well, isn't she?'

He nodded. 'Oh yes, she's fine, never better, and I feel lousy, talking about her like this. It's just that I can't shake off this feeling.'

'What feeling, Danny?' Robyn put her hand on his arm. 'You can tell me. I promise it won't go any further, and I might be able to help.'

He took a deep breath. 'Well, it's just that I can't help feeling she *likes* me like this – helpless.' His face coloured. 'Oh, damn! It sounds terrible put into words like that. It's just that I get the feeling that she's thinking of me as a baby again. She's actually looking forward to having me home, helpless and totally dependent on her like I was when I was little. I suppose it's being on her own,' he added unhappily.

'Oh, Danny!' It was as Robyn had suspected when she had first met Mrs Rawlings.

'I don't want you to think I'm complaining,' he told her quickly, his eyes grave and troubled. 'She's a wonderful mum and a lot of people would give their eye teeth for someone who'd actually *enjoy* looking after an invalid, but – but...'

'You don't have to explain. I know what you mean.' Robyn was thinking of David, her brother, and wondering why it was that in real life things never seemed to balance out properly. 'Is there anything I can do? Your mum and I have met. Would you like me to go and see her?'

His face brightened. 'Would you? Do you think you could find some way to get through to her that I needn't be helpless for the rest of my life? You see, I've heard of this place – it's a rehabilitation centre where I could go after they've done all they can for me at Ennermoor. I'd learn to look after myself and they'd teach me a craft or skill too so that I could earn my own living and be totally independent. It'd be easier for me than for a lot of people. I never had a job, so I haven't lost anything that way. I was always interested in art at school. Maybe I could do something in that line.' He frowned, his mouth puckering. 'But Mum thinks it's a waste of time. She wants me to go home and let her take care of me. Sometimes I feel...' He broke off, looking apologetically at

167

Robyn. 'Oh God, I feel so disloyal. Can you understand?'

'Of course I can, Danny. You mustn't feel disloyal. It is a problem and should be sorted out. Look, I'll go and see your mother as soon as I get the chance.' She patted his shoulder. 'And don't worry, I shan't tell her we've had this conversation. Anyway, I'm sure you're going to get on wonderfully at Ennermoor.'

He smiled. 'Got to face the facts, haven't I, Miss Seers? Chances are I'll be in a chair for the rest of my life, but I dare say there are worse things.'

On the drive back to Ravenshore Robyn was silent. Danny's courage and fortitude should have cheered her, but it had had the reverse effect. It seemed so cruel that he should be so resigned to his life in a wheelchair. One moment he had been full of youthful health and vitality, the next, his whole life lay in agonising ruins. She wasn't aware that she had spoken the last few words until Bill turned to look at her as they turned on to the coast road.

'That poor kid really gets to you, doesn't he?'

She nodded, her eyes filling with tears as she looked out over tossing, restless water.

This morning everything looked as grey and turbulent as the sea.

'Tell you what,' said Bill, 'I'll take you out for a slap-up lunch to make up for our ruined weekend.'

She turned to look at him and her mood lightened a little as she took in the comically hopeful face with its two black yes. 'You're joking! You can't go anywhere looking like that, Bill!' She laughed in spite of herself. 'You look like a panda!'

He sighed. 'Got to face people some time. I daresay I'll be getting some stick when I show up in the reporters' room on Monday!'

When Fay saw him she echoed Robyn's remark: 'Good grief! What in the world happened to you?' She looked at Robyn. 'What on earth have you been doing to him?'

'It's a long story and I reckon I'm going to be sick of telling it by this time next week,' Bill told her resignedly.

Robyn was silent, knowing that any story he would tell was likely to be a fabrication. He could hardly tell the truth; it was too humiliating.

Bill stayed to lunch with the two girls, persuaded by a kind-hearted Fay, who didn't press him to tell her what happened. After he had gone, insisting that a piece of steak he had back at the flat would get rid of the bruising round his eyes before Monday, Fay looked at Robyn.

'I hope you're not going to keep me in suspense any longer,' she said, head on one side. 'I've been dying of curiosity all through lunch.'

'It's a long story, as Bill said,' Robyn sighed. 'Longer than he realises.'

Fay put away the last of the dishes and filled the kettle. 'Curiouser and curiouser,' she said gleefully. 'I've had a really dull week, so a good story will be like manna from heaven. I'll make another pot of coffee and you can tell me all about it.' She turned to look at Robyn and the smile disappeared from her face.

'Oh, what is it, love? Something has gone badly wrong, by the look of it.'

'Oh, Fay, I've made a prize fool of myself!' A lump filled Robyn's throat and tears welled up in her eyes as she struggled with the words.

'Here, sit down. Look, don't mind me. Have a good howl if you feel like it.' Fay looked at her anxiously. 'And you don't have to tell me anything if you don't want to. I feel awful now, gloating over someone else's misfortune.'

Robyn swallowed and fumbled for a handkerchief. No one could be more kind-hearted or discreet than Fay. She was the last person to gloat, and she longed to pour the events of the previous day and night out to someone.

'To begin with, Bill had an ulterior motive for taking me to Windermere for the weekend,' she began.

Fay smiled wryly. 'Well, I guessed that!' Her mouth dropped open. 'Oh! Don't tell me *you*...'

Robyn shook her head. 'No, I didn't. And it wasn't what you think either.' She went on to relate the rest of the story, from Ross's fortuitous appearance at the Fox and Grapes last night to the message she had discovered on the answering machine this morning. When she had finished Fay shook her head.

'But if Ross had asked Fiona to marry him, surely he wouldn't have...'

'I imagine he was trying to prove something,' Robyn said quickly. 'After all, that ego of his must have taken a pretty hard battering when I walked out like that.' She lifted her shoulders resignedly. 'Well, he succeeded, didn't he? I hope he's satisfied.'

Fay looked at her helplessly. 'But – I thought you felt so strongly about the way he treated you.'

Robyn's hands were clenched tightly in her lap as she tried to analyse the events of the previous evening: 'I was there, alone with him late at night, for the first time in two years. I'd had more of that wretched brandy than I realised and – and…' The tears began again. 'Oh, Fay, I can't help it. It's no use trying to make excuses. I still love him, and it isn't making it any easier, knowing that all the things I've always suspected about him are right!'

'Look, just a minute,' Fay said slowly. 'Don't you think you should have waited – had it out with him?'

Robyn shook her head. 'How could I face the humiliation? I should have walked out the night before. That was the only way I could have escaped with any dignity. I made myself so – so *available!*' She began to walk round the room restlessly. 'I feel such a *fake!* Here I am, trying to help other people organise their lives, and I can't manage my own without making a mess of it!'

Fay shook her head. 'Don't, love. He isn't worth it.' She gave her friend a reassuring hug. 'Look, Robbie, I know it won't be easy, staying here and running into him constantly, but you do have friends here in Crownhaven, so please don't think of leaving again. Stay and face it out. Show him you don't care and maybe, some day soon, you'll find that you don't any more!'

Robyn knew it was good advice. She had made good friends since she had been here. Fay was right, it would be foolish to run away and face starting all over again.

The following week started busily, but on Wednesday morning she and Jim had a special assignment. They were to collect a patient from Crownhaven General and take him to Ennermoor Spinal Unit. That patient was Danny Rawlings. On the way there Jim glanced at Robyn.

'I might as well come clean, I volunteered us for this one. Thought you'd like me to.'

She shot him a grateful smile. 'Thanks, Jim. I dropped in to see Danny last Sunday, so I knew he was going soon. I think he's quite looking forward to it. He's got guts.'

'I hope you're not still blaming yourself,' said Jim. 'After all, you did save his life, you know.'

She nodded. 'I'm satisfied now that we did everything we could. And apparently there is still a small chance that he could get some of the use back in his legs.'

'Great! I'm glad.'

At the hospital they found Mrs Rawlings waiting. She was to accompany her son to Ennermoor and see him settled. Watching her shrewdly from a distance, Robyn could see what Danny had meant. She was solicitous to the point of fussiness, and Danny's patience grew short as she clucked around him, tucking in his blankets and holding his hand. Robyn made a mental note to arrange to have coffee with her in the near future so that they could have the talk she had promised Danny.

She got the opportunity later that morning, after they had seen Danny settled in his new environment.

'Have you a car, Mrs Rawlings?' she asked as they walked back to the ambulance. The other woman shook her head.

'No, but the bus service is fairly good and it stops right outside the hospital. I shall try to come every day.'

Robyn took a deep breath. 'I shouldn't if I were you.'

Mrs Rawlings looked shocked. 'But he'll be expecting me. I couldn't disappoint him.'

'Visiting every day is all right for short-term patients,' Robyn told her. 'Danny is

174

likely to be here for some time. Don't you think it would be better to give him the chance to make friends and settle into the routine – not rely on you so much?'

Danny's mother looked unconvinced and Robyn decided not to press the matter further for the time being. 'I'll tell you what,' she offered, 'I've promised to visit Danny too. I thought I'd come over on my next day off. Why don't we come together? It would save you a bus ride.'

'Oh, that *would* be nice.' Mrs Rawlings brightened. 'But you must let me treat you to tea afterwards.'

Robyn smiled. 'I think that would be very enjoyable. I'll ring you, shall I?'

Two days later, while she was in the Outpatients Department of Crownhaven General, Robyn found herself unexpectedly face to face with Fiona Muir. The physiotherapist came suddenly round the corner, almost bumping into Robyn as she was making her way towards the ENT clinic to pick up a patient.

'Hello there. How are you – and how is your friend?'

Robyn blushed guiltily as she looked into Fiona's smiling face. 'Oh, I'm fine, and so is

Bill. I think he had to put up with quite a bit of ribbing from colleagues at work, but apart from that he's made a good recovery.'

'I'm so glad. I never can think why black eyes are considered so funny,' Fiona said. 'I've never had once myself, but they look jolly painful. I take it Ross saw you home all right afterwards?'

Robyn wished fervently that there was something she could do to stop the rich colour from flooding into her cheeks. 'Oh yes – thanks.' She moistened her dry lips. 'I – er – take it that congratulations are in order.'

For a moment the other girl looked taken aback, then she smiled. 'Ross told you, then? Well, you are old friends, aren't you? I expect he also told you that we don't want it known for a while. I'm sure you'll respect that.'

'Of course,' Robyn said bleakly.

'It's just that nothing is finally settled and we don't want too many people asking questions yet.' Fiona smiled. 'It's exciting, though, isn't it?'

'It must be, yes.' Robyn looked at her watch. 'I'd better go and pick up my patient now.'

'Nice to see you again,' said Fiona. 'And

tell Fay I'm looking forward to coming over to Ravenshore to see the cottage. Maybe I'll bring Ross with me. 'Bye!'

She disappeared round the corner, leaving Robyn stunned. So it was true, then. The idea of entertaining the newly engaged couple to tea at Fell Cottage filled her with horror. She must think up an excuse to be out when the time came.

She had neither seen nor heard from Ross since the morning when she had walked out of his flat. And when Fiona came to Fell Cottage to tea the following Sunday afternoon Robyn didn't have to think up an excuse to be out. She was on duty. She arrived home at six o'clock and saw with dismay that the long white E-type was still parked outside. Her heart sank. Would Ross be with her? What would she say to him?

Steeling herself, she let herself in with her key, holding her breath as she listened carefully to the buzz of conversation coming from the living-room. There seemed to be only the two feminine voices, and she heaved a sigh of relief, pushing open the door. The other two girls looked up.

'Good, you're in time to save us making pigs of ourselves over this gâteau,' Fay smiled. 'Tea? I expect you're dying for a cup as usual.'

Robyn sat down gratefully, accepting the cup Fay handed her along with a slice of rich-looking Black Forest gâteau on a plate. She was acutely aware of Fiona's eyes on her; of her scrubbed face and uniform, starkly contrasting with the other girl's elegantly cut suit and flawless make-up.

'I do like that shade of French navy,' Fiona said sincerely. 'It really suits you, Robyn. I think the ambulance service uniform is quite smart.' Then, as though sensing her unasked question: 'By the way, Ross couldn't come. He said he had some paperwork to catch upon on. I daresay he would have been bored with our girlish chatter anyway.' She smiled. 'I saw an admirer of yours the other day. He sent his regards.'

Robyn looked up. 'Oh? Who was that?'

'Danny Rawlings. I went over to Ennermoor to help out. He's doing fine – already talking about going to a rehabilitation centre. I was telling him about the one I worked at for a time. It was down in Hampshire – Meadowlands.'

'Oh yes, I believe I've heard of it,' said Robyn.

'He wouldn't qualify for that, though, unfortunately,' Fiona went on. 'It's for disabled people who have no relatives. Danny has his mother, of course. It seems she can't wait to have him home. He's lucky.'

Robyn shrugged. 'As long as she doesn't make him too dependent on her.'

'Oh, I don't think there's any fear of that.' Fiona was thoughtful. 'Some of the cases I saw at Meadowlands were really tragic – like the young man paralysed in a car accident whose wife had walked out on him.' She looked up. 'By the way, *that* was where I heard your name before. It was the same as this young chap's. Seers – David Seers.'

There was a crash as Robyn's cup and saucer hit the floor. 'Oh!' she gasped. 'Oh – I'm sorry. I'll get a cloth.' She jumped up and ran out of the room, her face ashen. Fiona looked at Fay.

'She looked as if she'd seen a ghost! Did I say something?'

By the time Robyn had cleared up the mess, Fiona had thanked Fay and driven off, explaining that she had promised to have dinner with her father that evening. Fay joined Robyn in the kitchen where she was washing out the floor cloth.

'Are you all right, love?' she asked quietly.

Robyn forced a smile. 'I'm fine. Sorry about the carpet, but I don't think it'll stain.'

179

Fay regarded her for a moment, remembering the way her colour had faded when Fiona had mentioned the patient with the same name. She would have liked to ask why, but chose to mind her own business for the moment.

'By the way,' she said, 'Fiona said nothing about her engagement, though I thought she might. I even threw out one or two gentle hints, but not a word! She did let slip one interesting piece of information, though. That block of flats where Ross St Clair lives belongs to her. It was part of the legacy her grandmother left her. Maybe they're planning to live there after they're married.'

During the days that followed Robyn had a great deal to think about. Everything pointed to the fact that Fiona and Ross were to be married, but now another matter pressed on her mind too. What should she do now that she knew her brother was alone again? Fiona hadn't mentioned how long ago she had been at Meadowlands Rehabilitation Centre, but she felt sure they would know where he was. She hated to think of him alone and maybe needing her. But perhaps it was all a mistake; perhaps there *was* another David Seers, paraplegic as the result of an accident. The answers to all her questions were as close as the nearest telephone, and yet she wasn't sure if she was strong enough to take the disappointment if the man in question wasn't David. And so each day came and went without her having done any more about it.

It was on Thursday, the last day of her stint on middle shift, when she and Jim were called out to an incident involving a young child. The mother had been too incoherent with anxiety to give full details, but it was clearly a case of extreme urgency.

They arrived at the little terraced house to find the door open and the hall full of well-meaning neighbours, all trying to give the child's mother advice. With his air of calm authority, Jim asked them to leave, though one woman was openly abusive.

'I'm going to ring for a doctor,' she said in a loud voice. 'These people are no more than van drivers! What do they know?'

But Jim failed to rise to the bait, ushering them firmly out into the street while Robyn pushed her way through to the living-room at the back of the house.

The child's mother met her, her eyes wide with fear as she handed Robyn the small, limp body of her three-year-old son.

181

'I think he's dead,' she whispered. 'He isn't breathing. Oh, *please* – is there anything you can do?'

Robyn took the child from her and laid him gently on the floor. At once she could see from the boy's darkened colour that he had stopped breathing. Jim was already hurrying out to the ambulance for the necessary equipment, including oxygen and suction apparatus.

Robyn could still feel a faint pulse in the child's neck and when she opened the tiny mouth and inserted her finger into the throat she found what she had expected, an obstruction. Swiftly she went into action. Grasping the instrument handed to her by Jim, she inserted it and located the opening to the windpipe. Peering in, she could clearly see the cause of the trouble. It looked like a large sweet of some kind. Jim handed her a pair of forceps, and very carefully Robyn gripped the slippery object, dislodged and removed it, then, removing the instrument quickly, she tipped the child's head back-wards and pinched his nostrils, applying mouth-to-mouth resuscitation. After a few breaths the child's colour began to improve and he began to breathe on his own. He regained consciousness and opened his eyes, rewarding them all with a healthy-sounding yell. The danger was over.

The child and his mother clung to each other, weeping noisily, and Jim smiled at Robyn across the two heads. After he had given them a moment or two to comfort each other he patted the woman's shoulder.

'Give the kiddie to me now, love. Let him have a rest to recover from the shock. Why don't you go and put the kettle on? You look as though you could do with a good strong cuppa.' When the woman didn't move he took the child gently from her and gave him to Robyn, then, taking the woman by the arm, he led her towards the door.

'Come on, let me give you a hand.'

Robyn laid the little boy on the settee and made him comfortable with cushions, talking reassuringly to him. She was just getting to her feet when a movement in the doorway made her look up, and her heart stood still when she found herself looking into Ross's grey eyes. It was the first time they had come face to face since that Saturday morning at his flat.

'Oh!' she exclaimed.

He looked at the child. 'I take it the emergency is over.'

'Yes – a bad case of choking. I managed to

remove the object.'

'Good.' He came into the room and opened his bag. 'Now I'm here I may as well check him over,' he said, taking out his stethoscope. 'I think it was an anxious neighbour who called me.'

By the time Ross had pronounced the child fit, the mother had reappeared from the kitchen with the tray of tea, insisting that they all took a cup and by the time they left the small boy was once again taking an interest in his toys on the floor, his close shave mercifully forgotten.

Outside, as Jim climbed into the ambulance's driving seat, Ross laid a hand on Robyn's arm.

'I want to talk to you.' His face was serious, almost grim.

She shook her head. 'No, not again, Ross.'

'What time are you free today?'

Anger quickened her heart. 'Don't you *ever* listen to what I say?'

'Your partner is waiting. What time?'

His fingers were tight around her arm. Jim was already looking curious. She felt trapped as she said quickly: 'Six, but I...'

'Where will you be?' he asked, glancing towards the ambulance. He shook her arm impatiently. 'Oh, come *on*, Robyn. You're holding us all up! Just name a place.'

Confused, she stammered out: 'The Blue Parakeet – it's a café in the High Street.'

'Right, I'll be there.' Ross was gone before she had time to think about the meeting she'd arranged. A moment later as she was climbing into her seat next to Jim, the sleek black car roared past them, Ross's eyes looking straight ahead. Jim looked at her with a quizzical grin.

'Hello, hello, hello! What's all this 'ere, then?'

Robyn shrugged. 'Just something he wanted for his records – about the case.'

Jim looked at her speculatively as she gazed abstractedly out of the window. All he said was: 'Speaking of which, hadn't you better radio Control that we're available and start writing up the report?'

Robyn tried hard not to think about the coming meeting as the afternoon progressed. How could she have allowed herself to be tricked into agreeing to meet Ross? And what could he possibly have to say to her? She could, of course, fail to turn up. But she knew Ross well enough to know that if she didn't appear he would probably turn up at the cottage demanding to know why, and she didn't want that.

They were on their way back to Control to sign off when the call came over the radio.

'All vehicles to go to Oddling's Chemical Works in Dock Street. Dangerous gases escaping. Multiple casualties.'

Jim's foot pressed hard down on the accelerator as he swung the vehicle round a U-turn. They were only two streets away from Dock Street and were the first to arrive on the scene. Complete chaos met them. A fire engine stood on the forecourt of the works, which was full of casualties in varying stages of collapse. Robyn and Jim could hear them coughing and gasping for breath, their eyes streaming in reaction to the evil fumes that had attacked them.

A fireman ran up as they drew to a halt. He wore a respirator, but he pulled it off to speak to them:

'No need for respirators, the escape is under control. You can go in, but most of the casualties are out here.'

They both jumped down from the vehicle and went quickly into action, collecting oxygen equipment from the ambulance and assembling stretchers for the more severe cases. The industrial nurse employed by Oddling's had done all she could, though she was clearly affected herself, and after

Jim had checked her she insisted on going to work with them, helping them to get the more urgent cases into the ambulance.

Soon the two-tone sirens of other ambulances could be heard as they converged on the scene. A foreman, one of the more slightly affected victims, was telling his story to Jim.

'The consignment was late – sulphuric acid. The tanker broke down.' He paused to draw a rasping breath. 'The driver rang in. I took the call – told him to leave the delivery until tomorrow, but he wouldn't have it – said he'd lose a day's pay if he did. He arrived just as the shifts were changing and started to unload the stuff into the wrong container. By the time I realised what was happening it was too late. The whole place was full of fumes!'

Jim put a hand on his shoulder. 'OK, no more talking. I'm sure you did all you could, mate.'

They and the other crews worked hard, dealing with everything from temporary blindness to severe chest pains and choking. It took them two hours to administer first aid and shuttle to and fro, ferrying the cases to Crownhaven General. When they were finished there was the report to write up.

Back at Control, Robyn showered and changed into her own clothes, then, at Jim's suggestion, stopped over after signing off to have an off-duty coffee at the canteen. It was as she raised her cup and took a long drink of the much needed liquid that her eye caught the clock. It was ten to nine. Almost three hours after the time she had arranged to meet Ross!

CHAPTER EIGHT

Robyn had bypassed the lift and walked up the ten flights of stairs to Ross's flat. She told herself it was to give herself time to think out what to say, but if she had been honest she would have admitted that once she got to the wrought-iron lift gates her nerve had failed her. She was really stalling for time – anything to put off the moment of coming face to face with him.

She was slightly breathless as she rang the bell and in the pause that followed she wrestled with her conflicting thoughts; the weaker half hoped that Ross would be out, while the stronger remained stubbornly defiant. It wasn't her fault that she hadn't turned up for the meeting he had insisted on last night. She wouldn't be blamed for something she couldn't help!

When he opened the door he looked surprised. 'Robyn!'

She came straight to the point. 'I wanted to explain why I didn't show up at the Blue Parakeet last night. There was an...'

'I know all about it,' he interrupted. 'I took an extra surgery this morning to help treat some of the less severe cases.'

'Oh – yes, of course.' Robyn took an uncertain step backwards. He hadn't asked her in. 'I – just thought you might think...'

'That you'd run out on me again?' he supplied, his eyebrows lifting a fraction. 'I should be getting used to that by now.' He stood aside. 'You can come in. At your own risk, of course,' he added, his lip curling sardonically.

She stepped past him into the flat. 'I thought I'd better come,' she said. 'To see what it was you wanted to talk about. It sounded important.'

He led the way through to the lounge, indicating a chair. 'Can I give you a drink? Or would you like some tea?'

She shook her head. 'It isn't really a social call, Ross. You said you wanted to talk to me. I didn't want you to think I was trying to avoid you.'

He inclined his head slightly. 'I assume you're ready to explain, in that case.'

'Explain what?'

His patience snapped and his eyes darkened angrily. 'Oh, for God's sake, Robyn! Stop playing games and come to the point, can't you? You want to tell me why you walked out the other morning and I want to hear it, so get on with it, can't you?' He looked at his watch. 'This is supposed to be my day off and I'd like to spend what's left of it pleasantly if possible!'

His tone stung her and she felt her colour rising. '*You* said you wanted to talk, not me.'

'All *right* – so why are we wasting time?'

For a moment they stared at each other. It was stalemate. Robyn looked miserably down at her hands, clenched in her lap.

'Just tell me what you were trying to prove?' she said. 'It was a pretty low trick, getting me up here, giving me brandy when you knew it would go to my head and then – then...'

'What the *hell* are you suggesting!' Ross was on his feet, really angry now as he crossed the room and stood menacingly over her; his eyes like granite as they glared down. 'Just what are you accusing me of, Robyn – *rape?*'

She sprang up and took a step backwards. 'No!'

'When I left the flat you were perfectly all right,' he went on. 'You'd even agreed to spend the day here. I get back to find a curt note waiting for me. I want an explanation.

I don't think that's unreasonable.'

Her eyes narrowed. He was doing it again; the thing he was so good at, turning the tables. She threw her head back. 'No! *I* want an explanation,' she told him. 'Let's take things in the proper order, shall we? You tell me why you made love to me – *then* I'll tell you why I left.'

When he didn't answer she seized on the silence. 'I'll tell you why, shall I?' Her heart was beating fast now. All the courage she had lacked before seemed to surge into her and the words poured out in a torrent.

'You want to have your cake and eat it, just like you always did!' she flung at him. 'It's that damned ambition of yours, isn't it? Fiona has so much more than mere *love* to offer, hasn't she? All that money – all that social clout, not to mention her father's practice! Saudi Arabia paid off in a way you never imagined it would, didn't it? You landed on your feet, as always. But when you found yourself alone with me again that night you just couldn't resist getting your own back, could you? Paying me out for deflating your blasted ego!'

Her eyes blazed up at him, her breast rising and falling rapidly with the quickened beat of her heart. His own eyes were hard and expressionless as they returned her furious gaze.

'Have you quite finished?' he asked. His voice was dangerously low and she knew from experience that he was using every ounce of self-control to curb his temper. She was past caring.

'I think so!'

'I've never heard such garbled rubbish in my life, and I can't think where you got it from,' he said scathingly. 'But if you think I'm about to start defending myself to you, then you've another think coming! The truth is something that never interested you much anyway. You've always preferred your own twisted version of things, especially when it was anything to do with me.'

'That's just your way of getting out of it,' she sneered. 'You wouldn't know what truth was if it sat up and sang to you! You have no integrity, Ross. I was right about you all along. If you've taken Fiona in too, then I'm – I'm *sorry* for her!'

His hands shot out to grasp her shoulders, his fingers hard as they sank into her flesh.

'All right! You've asked for it and now you're going to get it. Why don't you start facing up to a few truths yourself for a change?'

'I – don't know what you mean,' Robyn faltered.

'You don't? Then I'll tell you. To begin with, you are certainly *not* in love with that – that small-time reporter, Hughes. If you were you wouldn't have responded to me as eagerly as you did!' Ross's eyes narrowed. 'I don't know though, you're devious enough even for that. It appears now that there was another man in your life even when we were together!' He shook his head at her. 'You're so close, Robyn. Even your right hand doesn't know what your left is doing! And you accuse *me* of being devious!'

'At least I don't let ambition rule my life!' she blazed at him, her heart hammering in her chest. 'I don't step on people's faces to get what I want!'

'Oh no? What do *you* call it, then? Tell me that?' He shook her as though she were a rag doll.

She put both hands against his chest and pushed with all her strength. 'Leave me alone! How *dare* you...'

'Oh! – I'm sorry, I couldn't make anyone hear and the door was unlocked, so I came in.'

They hadn't heard her footsteps on the thick carpet and they both stopped dead,

194

turning to stare at the owner of the voice. Fiona stood in the doorway, looking curiously from one to the other.

Ross made a rapid recovery. 'Fiona! I'm sorry, I didn't hear you. Come in. Robyn was just leaving. She came to tell me about the incident at Oddling's Works yesterday afternoon.' His arm across Robyn's shoulders looked deceptively casual, but Robyn felt the hardness of his fingers as he escorted her firmly to the door. She looked at Fiona over her shoulder as she passed, attempting to smile.

'Goodbye.'

'Please don't hurry away because of me.' Fiona looked perplexed as she stared after them.

It was only when Robyn found herself outside with the door firmly closed on her that she registered the fact that Fiona had been carrying a suitcase. Clearly she was moving in!

'Well, I wish her joy of him,' she muttered under her breath as she began the long descent. But by the time she reached the street below, her temper had cooled, dampened by the tears that stung her eyes and constricted her throat.

The first snow of the winter was falling as Robyn drew up outside the Rawlings' house on the following Tuesday afternoon. When Mrs Rawlings opened the door she was obviously ready but full of misgivings.

'You don't think the roads are going to get bad, do you? I don't want you to take any risks because of us.'

Robyn smiled. 'I've driven in some pretty bad conditions, Mrs Rawlings. It's only a few flakes, I don't think it'll be much.'

The older woman followed her out to the car and got in. 'Well, we'll see,' she said, peering doubtfully through the windscreen. 'I'll tell you what, instead of having tea out, maybe it would be a better idea if you came back to the house. I did a batch of baking this morning.'

Robyn let in the clutch and pulled away from the kerb. 'That sounds fine. Thank you very much.' She glanced at her passenger. 'Have you seen Danny lately? How does he seem to be settling in?'

Mrs Rawlings shook her head. 'He seems happy enough, but I do feel they're a little hard with him. They expect him to do an awful lot for a boy who's so helpless. It doesn't seem right, somehow.'

'I'm sure they wouldn't ask more than he's

capable of,' Robyn assured her. 'Danny is young and very strong – that's what pulled him through his illness. He has all his life before him. It would be very sad if he gave up, don't you think?'

Mrs Rawlings sighed. 'I suppose you're right, but I can't help wishing I could have him home where I could look after him myself.' She looked at Robyn. 'You must know how I feel, having had a brother in the same situation. You must have felt the same – that you wanted to do all you could to help him.'

Robyn was silent, staring through the flurries of snow at the road ahead. The woman beside her spoke again.

'Tell me, how did you cope with it – the helpless feeling, trying not to fuss too much?'

'I didn't get the chance to find out, Mrs Rawlings,' Robyn said abruptly. 'What I didn't tell you that day in the cafeteria was that I lost all contact with my brother on the day I left to begin my training. His wife told me they didn't want to see me again. She blamed me for the accident, you see. I felt I should leave them to adjust, but I think she felt I was opting out. I realise now that she felt trapped and resented me.'

Mrs Rawlings looked shocked. 'Oh, my

dear! And your brother...?'

Robyn shrugged. 'I don't know. I wrote, of course, but the letters all came back unopened. Christmas and birthday cards too.' She glanced at her passenger. 'That's why I don't talk about it.'

Mrs Rawlings was shocked into silence and Robyn went on: 'Quite by chance I heard something about him the other day. I believe I know where I can get in touch again. If my information is correct David is on his own now. It seems his marriage broke up after all. I don't quite know what to do about it.'

Mrs Rawlings laid a hand on her arm. 'Oh, but you must get in touch. If there's the slightest chance he might want to see you again, you *must* try. After all, it was his wife who rejected you, wasn't it?'

'I'm so afraid there might be some mistake, though,' Robyn explained. 'The name is fairly uncommon but not all that much so. I don't think I could bear it if I summoned up my courage for nothing.'

But by the time they drove in through the gates of Ennermoor Hospital Robyn had made a decision: she would ring Meadowlands this evening. Maybe the David Seers Fiona had met *was* a different person –

198

maybe they would refuse to divulge information about patients on the telephone. But Mrs Rawlings was right, she had to try.

They found Danny in great spirits. He had been undergoing extensive tests and having daily physiotherapy to improve the muscle tone lost during his long period of inactivity. Already he was taking an active part in the wheelchair sports and other recreations organized at the unit, and he seemed to be enjoying himself enormously.

Robyn watched Mrs Rawlings closely during the visit and thought she seemed wistful. When it was time to leave she clung to Danny just a fraction too long, and Robyn saw the boy try hard not to look irritated.

'Leave it out, Mum,' he said, his freckled face colouring as he glanced round. 'You don't want me labelled a mother's boy, do you?'

His mother looked hurt as she glanced round at the other patients. 'Some of the others in here look a little on the rough side, Danny,' she whispered. 'I know you're all in the same boat, but I don't think it's wise to make friends with just *anyone*, do you?'

Danny frowned. 'You don't have a chance to think that way in here,' he told her. 'Disablement is a great leveller. If you didn't try to get on with people you'd have a pretty miserable time.'

'Oh, I'm sorry for them all, of course,' his mother said quickly. 'It's just...'

Danny switched on a bright smile and turned to Robyn. 'Thank you for coming to see me, Miss Seers, and for bringing Mum. If you're up at the hospital some time, giving my best to all the nurses on MS, won't you?'

Mrs Rawlings was silent as they walked down the corridor, and it wasn't until they were in the car that she spoke. Looking at Robyn, she said unhappily:

'I meant to try so hard. I'm sorry if I embarrassed you.'

'You didn't.' Robyn would have liked to add that it was poor Danny who was embarrassed, but she had a pretty good idea that Mrs Rawlings already knew that. She turned in her seat and looked at the older woman.

'Look, you'll probably think this is a cheek, coming from a stranger and someone so much younger. But if I were you I'd let Danny set the pace from now on.'

Robyn held her breath as Mrs Rawlings stared at her. She'd really laid her head on the block, and if she was about to be told to

200

mind her own business it was no more than she'd asked for.

But Mrs Rawlings' face suddenly lost its defensive look and crumpled. 'I know,' she whispered. 'You're quite right, but I can't help wanting to protect him – after all, he's all I've got.' She fumbled in her handbag for a handkerchief and dabbed at her eyes.

Robyn felt she might have been unnecessarily brutal. She bit her lip, touching the other woman's arm. 'I'm sorry if that sounded cruel. And I know how you must feel.' She frowned, searching for a way to put into words what she wanted to say. 'I've seen a lot of people hurt in accidents, Mrs Rawlings. Often I never see them again, but sometimes we get to follow them up – taking them for physiotherapy and so on, during their recovery. I can tell you one thing: it can either make or break a person's character, and a lot depends on the attitude of their families. It seems to be that Danny is coping superbly. He's a courageous man and you have every right to be proud of him. But you *must* let him do it his own way.'

Mrs Rawlings shook her head. 'He's only a child – a boy.'

'No!' Robyn's fingers tightened on the arm she touched. 'Danny is a *man*, and it's

201

important for him to feel like one and for you to help him to. Don't you see?'

There was a long silence as the other woman wrestled with her feelings, then she turned suddenly and smiled at Robyn.

'You're right – I should have worked that out for myself. I would if I hadn't been blinded by my own emotions, I suppose.' She took Robyn's hand and squeezed it warmly. 'Promise me one thing?'

Robyn smiled. 'If I can. What?'

'That you'll try to get in touch with that brother of yours again. If he needs a friend he couldn't have a better one than you!' Mrs Rawlings took a deep breath, putting her handkerchief away in her handbag again. 'I'll tell you what, after we've had tea you can use my telephone, then you'll be sure you're not overheard.' She smiled conspiratorially. 'It'll be our secret.'

By the time Robyn left Mrs Rawlings' house that evening a thick blanket of snow covered everything. The afternoon's flurries had turned to a near blizzard, but now the sky had cleared and the moon was up, turning the landscape into a glittering wonderland. But Robyn's attention was concentrated more on the hazardous roads beneath the wheels of her car. As she drove she allowed her thoughts to go back over the events of the evening. After the superb high tea Mrs Rawlings had insisted on giving her the older woman had looked at her enquiringly.

'Well, how about making that call? You can do it while I wash up. No one will disturb you.'

Robyn's heart had missed a beat as she searched for yet another excuse to put off the fatal call.

'Oh, but I don't know the number.'

Mrs Rawlings smiled as she got up and began to clear the table. 'You know as well as I do that you have only to ring directory enquiries. Come along now, no time like the present.'

Robyn asked for the number and dialled it with shaking hands. A woman answered, and Robyn learned that she was Sister Grey, in charge of the Centre.

Briefly she explained who she was and what she wanted. She described David and Sister Grey admitted that it sounded very much as though they were speaking of the same person. But, as Robyn had suspected, it was the Centre's policy not to release details of patients over the telephone. Robyn's heart sank, then she had an idea.

203

'Would you do something for me?' she asked. 'Could you get in touch with him and tell him I rang? I'll give you my number, and then if he wants to contact me it'll be up to him.'

There was a pause at the other end of the line, then Sister Grey said: 'Well, I don't see why I shouldn't do that for you.'

'I'll confirm it in writing if you like,' Robyn added eagerly.

'I'm sure that won't be necessary. Just give me your full name and telephone number.'

Sister Grey had taken down the details, promising that she would pass them on. Now there was nothing to do but wait.

The snow brought forth its own spate of minor accidents, as Robyn had known it would, and the next few days were busy for her and Jim. Several elderly people living alone were admitted to hospital with bronchial complaints or hypothermia and there were the usual fractures and sprains caused through falls on slippery pavements. All these created a lot of paperwork, and by the end of the week Robyn had almost forgotten her call to Meadowlands the previous Tuesday.

It was on Friday evening when, weary after an especially chaotic shift, she was letting herself into the cottage. She could hear the phone ringing even before she opened the door, and she remembered with dismay that Fay was on late duty and would not be home until after eight. She sighed. The cottage felt cold and unwelcoming as she picked up the receiver, her coat half on and half off.

'Hello. Robyn Seers speaking.'

'Hello, Robbie. Long time no see.'

She dropped her shoulder bag on the floor and groped for a chair, her knees suddenly weak. 'David, is it really you?'

'You bet! It was a fantastic surprise for me when Sister Grey rang and said you'd been in touch.'

'Oh, David! Where are you? Can we meet? Are you all right?'

He laughed. 'I'm at Great Cottering in the Midlands. I've got a super flat and a job. I manage just fine, but it's a long story. As for meeting, I can't wait. I want to hear all your news.'

Robyn swallowed hard at the lump in her throat. 'I – heard about Mary. Is it true?'

'That we split up? Yes. Don't worry, it was a mutual decision. Some people are just no good in this situation. It was best for both of us.'

Robyn rummaged in her bag for paper and pencil. 'Give me your address and tell me how to get there. I'll come down.'

'No,' he told her firmly, 'I'll come up there to see you. I have a specially adapted car and I'm totally independent. If you could just find me somewhere to stay. I do have problems getting through normal doors.' He chuckled. 'Some people maintain it's my head that's the trouble!'

Robyn was about to argue, then she remembered the advice she had given Mrs Rawlings and stopped just in time.

'All right, then. When will you come?'

'Next weekend OK?'

'Fine.'

'Right. Tell me how to get there, then.'

Speaking to her brother had given Robyn a fresh burst of energy, and she sang as she set about preparing supper for herself and Fay. She lit the fire in the living-room and by the time the other girl arrived, the cottage was warm and welcoming, a blazing wood fire crackling merrily on the hearth and an appetising smell of cooking coming from the kitchen.

Over supper Robyn told her all about David and how she had found him again. It took quite some time. When she had finished

Fay sat back and surveyed her friend for a long time.

'Well, I must say you're a dark horse,' she said at last. 'But I'm glad something nice has happened for you. You've had quite a time of it one way and another lately, haven't you?'

Robyn nodded, stretching happily. 'I've been thinking, I might give up here after all and go down to the Midlands.'

Fay stared at her in dismay. 'You wouldn't! After all you said?'

'Ah, I wouldn't move in with David or try to organise him in any way,' Robyn told her quickly. 'I daresay I could find a job with the Ambulance Service down there. It's just that David is all I've got and it would be nice to be near him. There's nothing for me up here, after all, is there? The row Ross and I had last week proved pretty conclusively that we can't even be friends any more. Besides, there's Fiona.'

Fay sighed, looking at her friend's wistful expression. 'I thought you were happy here, in spite of everything.' She glanced at her friend. 'What about Bill?'

Robyn shook her head. 'Bill's fun, but I know now that I could never feel anything deep for him.' She sighed. 'You know, in his way he's as bad as Ross.'

'I'll certainly miss you if you do decide to go,' said Fay with a sigh.

'I'd miss you too,' Robyn assured her. 'But I feel that while Ross is here I'm always going to be crossing swords with him.' She looked up. 'It hurts, and I can't see that changing.'

For a long moment Fay was silent, then she smiled. 'Of course – I do see how difficult it must be for you. I'm just selfish, wanting you to stay.' She got up from the table. 'Now I'm going to do the washing-up. You sit by the fire and have a look at the evening paper – I got one on my way home.' She took it out of her bag and gave it to Robyn. 'I'll make coffee when I've finished. Go on, put your feet up.'

Robyn did as she was told gratefully. As she opened the *Courier* her thoughts turned again to Bill. She hadn't seen him for days and she wondered what he had been doing. He must have been busy not to have telephoned her. One look at the front page told her why.

New Health Centre For Crownhaven, the banner headline read. Below, the article told of the exposure of secret plans for a smart new health centre in the town which would house every branch of the medical profession from chiropodists to dentists; even embracing some of the fringe practitioners such as osteopaths and acupuncturists. Robyn read on with interest, wondering where Bill had got all his information from. Then suddenly her heart gave a jolt as she noticed a name near the end of the article.

The brains behind this exciting new scheme is Dr Ross St Clair, a popular and comparatively new GP. It went on to report on Ross's previous career in London and his high qualification for the post, but Bill had added a controversial sting in the tail that was likely to cause a furore:

But before we get too excited about the plan we must ask ourselves one very important question: Can Crownhaven afford such costly experiments? How high will our rates have to climb to allow ambitions of this kind to be satisfied? As plans for the project are unlikely to be turned down, only time will tell!

Robyn dropped the paper as though it were red-hot. This time Bill had gone too far, much too far! It seemed she had made her decision to leave Crownhaven just in time.

But it seemed that even in that she was wrong. The girls were just finishing their coffee when there was a ring at the bell.

They looked at each other.

'Are you expecting anyone?' asked Fay. Robyn shook her head.

'No, but I'll go. I wonder who it can be.'

She went into the hall and switched on the light. When she opened the door she was surprised to find Fiona waiting impatiently to be admitted. Robyn smiled, opening her mouth to greet her, but one look at the other girl's face froze the words on her lips.

'May I come in?' Fiona asked icily.

'Of course.' Robyn stood aside to admit her, then closed the door quickly. There was a cold wind blowing in from the sea, but an even colder one emanated from Fiona as she stared down at her.

'What can we do for you? I expect you want Fay,' said Robyn.

'You're wrong. It's you I want!'

Fiona pulled a copy of the *Courier* out from under her arm and waved it under Robyn's nose.

'How dare you disclose something told to you in strict confidence?' she demanded. 'It's quite unforgivable. I thought you were supposed to be an old friend of Ross's! He's going to be absolutely furious when he finds out about this leak, I can tell you!'

CHAPTER NINE

Fay handed Fiona a cup of coffee, glancing at Robyn as she did so.

'Here, drink this and tell us exactly what happened, Fiona. Start at the beginning. I'm finding it all rather confusing.'

Fiona took a sip of her coffee, looking at Robyn apologetically over the rim of the cup.

'I'm sorry I sounded off at you like that, Robyn,' she said. 'It's just that when I saw the paper this evening, I blew my top. We wanted to keep the plans for the new health centre under wraps – announce it at the right time when we could answer all the questions that are bound to be asked. Now it seems someone has leaked it to the press.' She lifted her shoulders. 'Knowing that Bill Hughes was a friend of yours and also that Ross had told you about the plans, I naturally put two and two together.'

'But Ross *didn't* tell me about it,' Robyn insisted.

'I know, so you said, and of course, I

211

believe you.' Fiona looked into her cup, finding it difficult to explain her doubts. 'It's just that you gave me the impression that he had when you congratulated me that day at the hospital.'

Robyn felt as though a cold hand had closed over her heart. Of *course*, she remembered now. She had congratulated Fiona on impulse, referring to her engagement and not realising that she was giving herself away. How could she explain now that she had heard the message on the answering machine, meant for Ross's ears only? On the other hand, how could she not?

She looked up to find the eyes of both girls on her, waiting, and a warm colour flushed her cheeks as she searched her mind feverishly for inspiration, then Fay said suddenly:

'I expect Robyn was talking about your engagement. I think she guessed, from something that was said, only she didn't like to say so.'

Robyn held her breath, hardly daring to look at Fiona. The other girl drew in her breath sharply.

'Well! I give you top marks for perceptiveness, Robyn. I'd barely made up my own mind at the time! And I can't think what I can have said to give myself away.' She frowned. 'But this isn't getting us any nearer to who leaked the information about the new health centre to the press.'

'Newspaper reporters are clever at getting that kind of information,' said Fay. 'It's all part of the job. Bill knows all kinds of people. There are a dozen places he might have got it from.'

'I suppose so.' Fiona got up, looking at her watch. 'Well, I must go.' She looked down at Robyn as she pulled on her gloves. 'I'm sorry again, Robyn. I hope we're still friends?'

Robyn smiled. 'Of course.'

Fiona stopped in the doorway. 'Oh, by the way, I didn't tell you, I've moved. I'm at Parkside Mansions now. Here's my new telephone number.' She opened her bag and took out a card which she dropped on to the table.

Fay showed Fiona out, coming back into the living-room to find Robyn looking pensive.

'That was a nasty moment.'

'I know. Thanks for getting me off the hook. I just didn't know what to say. For one thing, I couldn't tell her I'd heard her private message on Ross's answering machine, and for another, I don't suppose she'd have been altogether delighted to know I'd spent the night at her fiancé's flat.' She clenched her fists. 'Oh, *damn* Ross St Clair! *Now* do you see that it's impossible for me to stay here?'

Fay admitted grudgingly that she did.

The snow seemed to have made most people think of Christmas, and at the Control Centre everyone was anxiously looking at the duty roster to see how much time they would be able to spend with their families this year. Robyn heard one young married man complaining. He had only recently become a father and it seemed he would not be at home with his new family to celebrate. On impulse she heard herself say:

'I'll do your Christmas Day shift for you, Chris, if you'll swap this Sunday's duty with me. My brother's coming for the weekend and I'd like to spend some time with him.'

The young man stared at her, his face incredulous. 'Of course I will! But are you sure – about Christmas, I mean; don't you want to go home or anything?'

She smiled and shook her head. 'This is as much my home as anywhere. Anyway, I daresay it'll be fairly quiet, and if I know anything about the Control Centre at Christmas we'll have a great time.'

'Well, if you're really sure...' He tried hard to sound doubtful, but he couldn't quite keep the look of delight off his face. Robyn felt a glow of satisfaction. At least she had done one good thing. Lately her life seemed to be one long disaster. If it weren't for the fact that she was to see David again this weekend life would be bleak indeed.

She had given a lot of thought to accommodation for David, but it had been Danny Rawlings who came up with the answer when she visited him on her day off.

'They always keep a bed here for visiting paras,' he told her. 'And they quite like success cases. Do you think he'd give us a talk about his experiences?'

'I'm sure he would, Danny. That's a great idea,' Robyn said excitedly. 'I'll see Sister on my way out.'

It was all arranged. Sister confirmed that they did indeed keep a room for disabled visitors and that it would be free this weekend. She asked about David and was interested to hear how independent he had become.

'I'm sure it will do the other patients good to hear his story,' she told Robyn with a smile. 'And I promise we won't monopolise him too much!'

The week progressed without anything too dramatic happening until Friday afternoon. Robyn and Jim were waiting outside the Outpatients Department of Crownhaven General for a group of elderly patients who were receiving physiotherapy. It was a grey afternoon. The snow had turned to slush and it had been raining, so that they were glad of the warmth inside the vehicle as they sat chatting.

'Why do you stay here, Robbie?' Jim asked suddenly. 'I'd say you were wasted, unless you intend to try for an instructor's job. In a larger town you could concentrate on your paramedic skills and get more experience.'

Robyn smiled. 'This has been good experience too. I like being involved with people, and you can't say I haven't broken ground for Women's Lib at Crownhaven.' She laughed. 'Before I came I think they viewed ambulancewomen rather like an elephant riding a bicycle! You know, what's the quote? It's not amazing that it does it well, as much as that it does it at all!'

Jim laughed with her. 'Well, I think I can safely say that you've blown *that* one sky high. Seriously though, why did you choose Crownhaven?'

She shrugged noncommittally. 'It's a long story, Jim. Anyway, I've been seriously thinking of giving in my notice after Christmas. My brother is in the Midlands. His marriage has broken up and I'd quite like to move nearer to him.'

He looked at her. 'I didn't even know you had a brother.'

'Yes. He's disabled – paraplegic. An accident,' she told him succinctly.

'Ah, well, I see...' He stopped speaking as he spotted their patients coming out of the building; starting the engine and pulling up to the Outpatients entrance. He smiled at Robyn as she prepared to get out and help the patients into the vehicle.

'Well, another shift nearly over,' he told her with a grin. 'Once we've dispatched this little lot safely we can get back to Control and sign off, thank goodness!'

But Jim might have known better than to tempt fate. They had just pulled up at the traffic lights in the busiest part of town. The street was bustling with Friday afternoon shoppers. Suddenly a man elbowed his way through the crowd and rushed up to them, waving his arms, his face red with exertion and anxiety.

'Oh, thank God! Can you help me?'

Jim wound down his window. 'What's the trouble?'

'We're working on an old building,' the man gasped. 'Just down there – Market Street. My mate has fallen from the roof.'

'We're not an emergency vehicle,' Jim explained. 'I'll radio Control for you if you like.'

'But you don't *understand!*' the man was panicking now. 'He's landed on some scaffolding about forty feet up. I can't tell how bad he is. He could slip and fall any minute. Can't you come?'

By now the lights had changed and impatient drivers behind them were sounding their hooters. Jim didn't argue.

'Better get in and direct us,' he said. 'Make it snappy.'

As they drove, following the man's directions, Robyn explained the situation to the passengers in the back, asking them to be patient. None of them raised any objection. Market Street was where Dr Muir and his partners had their group practice, and Jim remarked upon the fact as they drew up outside the partly restored building. He turned to the workman.

'Look, you show my partner here where your mate is. I can't leave the vehicle here, it's obstructing the traffic. When I've parked it out of the way I'll see if there's a doctor available at the surgery and have him standing by, in case we need him.'

Robyn grabbed the emergency satchel and got out, following the workman over rubble and bricks into the shell of the building. Standing in the centre, he pointed upwards.

'Look, there he is. Think you can make it up to him, miss? I'll help you.'

Robyn's heart took a nosedive. If there was one thing on earth she hated it was heights. She swallowed hard. The man's position looked precarious as he lay spreadeagled across the narrow scaffolding platform forty feet above. There was no way of knowing whether or not he was conscious from here, or how badly injured he might be.

'I'll try,' she said, slipping both arms through the strap of the satchel so that it was slung out of the way on her back. 'OK, I'm ready.'

She followed the man up ladders and along scaffolding without too much trouble, resisting the temptation to look down all the time, but when they reached the level of the injured man she received a shock. The only way to get to him was across a plank that led from one set of scaffolding to another. She looked at the man.

'That doesn't look too safe.'

'It is,' he assured her. 'We wheel barrows of bricks across. It's quite secure.'

For the first time Robyn looked down, and her heart almost stopped. The ground looked about a mile away. Below, several people had gathered, their faces pale blobs as they gazed upwards. Then she heard the injured man groan and knew that she had no choice.

Inch by inch she made her way across the plank. It gave alarmingly under her feet, and to make matters worse the rain had made it slippery. Her heart drummed loudly in her ears at every step and she tried not to think about how she was to get the injured man back. Maybe if he was very bad Jim would send for the fire brigade. All she could do was hope and pray.

At last she reached him, and as she crouched beside him he raised his eyes and looked at her.

'My God, a woman!' he muttered. 'A pretty one too. I'm not dreaming, am I?'

As Robyn eased the satchel off her back she quickly assessed him. He was pale and sweating in spite of the cold wind blowing up here; she could see by his chattering teeth that he was in pain and shocked too, as she would have expected. But at least he was conscious. That was something!

'Where have you hurt yourself?' she asked.

'Shoulder,' he told her, wincing with pain. 'Landed on it. Reckon it's broken – I felt it snap.'

She nodded. 'Hurt anywhere else?'

The man gave her a twisted grin. 'Might as well ask where it *don't* hurt. You name it, love!'

After easing off the man's jacket and making a brief examination Robyn satisfied herself that he was right when he had assumed that his arm was broken. There was a large swelling forming at the head of his left humerus, and by the way the arm hung uselessly at his side, she was pretty sure that the clavicle was broken too, which would account for the snapping he had described. But these seemed to be the worst of his injuries. At least his legs were intact, she told herself gratefully.

Gingerly helping him into a sitting position, she placed a thick pad under the arm and immobilised it with the broadest bandage she could find, securing his hand against the right shoulder. She looked at him. Now that he was upright it was clear that he was experiencing pain at the base of the neck, caused by the broken clavicle.

'What's your name?' she asked him as she secured the sling.

'Ron,' he told her between clenched teeth.

'OK, Ron, you're doing fine. Now look, we've got to get across the plank. Do you think you can make it? I know it's going to hurt, but your mate's waiting on the other side and we have a doctor standing by.'

He tried hard to smile. 'Don't have much choice, do I? I'll make it, love, don't worry.'

Very carefully Robyn helped him to his feet and on to the plank beside her, drawing a long sigh of relief. That was the first step over.

Inching their way together, they made slow progress back across the plank. It wasn't easy. Although he made light of it, Ron was clearly in great pain. He was severely bruised from his fall and Robyn knew that his arm and neck must be hurting unbearably. Her fear of heights was almost forgotten in her concern for him.

At last they reached the scaffolding on the other side and the waiting workman held out his arms eagerly.

'Careful how you handle him,' warned Robyn. 'He's got a broken arm and collarbone and he's badly bruised.'

It seemed an age before their feet touched solid ground again, and when she reached the bottom Robyn's legs felt like jelly. Jim was waiting with a trolley stretcher and warmed blankets.

'We're to take him to the surgery,' he told her. 'It's only up the road. It'll be warmer in there. I've parked the ambulance outside.'

'What about the patients?' Robyn asked as they made their patient comfortable.

'Control sent another team with the stretcher, and they took them.' He grinned. 'I think they were quite miffed. They wanted to watch you do your stuff.' He peered into her pale face. 'All right, Robbie love?'

She grinned wryly. 'Fine – now!'

At the surgery the receptionist told them to take the man to room three where Dr St Clair had just finished his surgery. They wheeled him in.

Ross got up from behind his desk and came to examine the man. He confirmed that he had fractured his left humerus and clavicle and was suffering from severe bruising and shock. Then he gave him a pain-killing injection and telephoned the hospital, advising that he was on his way and would need immediate attention, while

Jim went out to radio Control about their movements.

The patient grinned up at Ross. 'Got this little lady to thank that I'm here at all,' he told him. 'Proper little brick, she was.'

Ross turned to Robyn. '*You* went up there for him?' he asked her. Taking her arm, he drew her quietly aside, looking into her face with concern.

'Are you all right? You can't stand on a chair without getting dizzy! You said so yourself only the other day.'

Robyn felt her stomach suddenly churn.

'Excuse me.' One hand over her mouth, she stumbled from the room.

In the cloakroom next door to the surgery she was violently sick. Coming out a few minutes later with shaking knees, she found Ross waiting in the corridor for her. He looked at her white, dirt-streaked face and took out his handkerchief, dabbing the beads of perspiration from her forehead.

'Why didn't you tell your partner you suffer from vertigo?' he asked sternly.

'I *don't!*' she protested fiercely. 'And don't you dare tell him – he'll think I'm not up to the job.'

He gave her a wry smile. 'I don't think anyone could accuse you of that!'

She was just finishing her evening meal when the telephone rang. Fay got up from the table.

'Stay where you are. I've finished mine. Anyway, it's probably Alan, he said he might ring this evening.'

A moment later she came back into the kitchen. 'It's for you,' she said. 'Ross St Clair.'

Robyn shook her head. 'Tell him I'm out.'

'Sorry, I've already said you're here. I didn't think.' Fay lifted her shoulders helplessly and Robyn got up and went resignedly into the hall.

'Hello, Ross.'

'Robbie, are you all right?'

'I'm fine, why?'

'You weren't exactly *all right* this afternoon, were you? You looked like death.'

'Well, I'm fine now,' she told him firmly. 'And, Ross, if you tell anyone...'

'Oh, don't be so stuffy!' he said impatiently. 'It wouldn't hurt if people knew you were human once in a while, would it? I must say I found it reassuring!'

Robyn drew in her breath sharply. 'If you just rang to rub in my weaknesses...'

'Wait! Don't hang up.'

The urgency of his tone made her stop.

225

'What is it you want, then?'

'Believe it or not, I rang because I was worried about you,' he told her.

'I see. Well, now that you're satisfied – or maybe you aren't! Maybe you'd have preferred me to be lying in a swoon, sniffing smelling salts.'

'What are you doing this weekend?' he asked, ignoring her irony.

The breath caught in her throat. 'I'm busy.'

'I don't believe you.'

'Oh, well, that's tough, because it happens to be the truth.'

'What are you doing?'

'Mind your own damned business!'

'I suppose you're going out with Bill Hughes,' he said.

'You can suppose what you like, Ross,' she told him. 'I'm not free this weekend or any other – not to you anyway. And you'll no doubt be relieved to hear that I intend to leave here after Christmas. No place in the world is big enough to hold both of us.'

Ross laughed, 'You sound like an old James Cagney movie!'

She slammed down the receiver and walked back into the living-room.

'From now on, Fay, I don't speak to that

man any more,' she said – then burst into tears.

When she woke on Saturday morning, Robyn lay looking forward to the day ahead, trying hard not to think of yesterday. David had telephoned two days ago to say he hoped to be at Ennermoor by teatime. She was to meet him there.

Even the thought of seeing him again made her nervous. They had so much to talk about. Did David share his wife's view that she was to blame for his accident? Were he and Mary really parted for good? There was so much she wanted to know. Was he happy? Had he made new friends? Would he like her to move to the Midlands to be nearer to him, or had he learned to live without a sister after all this time?

She got up, showered and dressed and went in to work her morning shift. It was good to have plenty to occupy her mind.

Signing off at two o'clock, she hurried back to Ravenshore to change and snatch a bite to eat, all the time growing more and more nervous. It was ridiculous, she told herself, being nervous about meeting one's own brother. Yet David must surely be a very different person from the man she had grown up with. He had always been so athletic, playing football and cricket, swimming and rowing. He could never tolerate anything that slowed him up. How then would life confined to a wheelchair have affected his personality?

As she drove out to Ennermoor later that afternoon she was glad that the weather had improved. She hadn't liked the thought of David driving on icy roads, yet she wouldn't have dared to ring and put him off.

She was surprised to find that he had already arrived. When she knocked on the door of Sister's office she was told that he was in the ward, talking to the other paraplegic patients.

'I'll go along with you, shall I?' Sister suggested. 'He's already volunteered to give us a talk about his experiences this evening. We're going to have a bit of a party. You're invited too, naturally.'

For a few moments, Robyn stood in the ward entrance, watching him, unobserved. He hadn't changed at all; the same unruly fair hair and quick, blue-eyed smile; the same air of mischievous innocence about him. He didn't see her for a moment, then Danny Rawlings spotted her and waved. David followed his glance and his face lit up as he began to wheel his chair towards her.

'Well, if it isn't my kid sister!'

As she held out her hands to him she didn't know whether to laugh or cry. Suddenly it was as though they had never been apart.

He insisted on taking her out to tea, driving her in his own car. She was impressed by the way he handled it and himself. Obviously Meadowlands had done a good job. Over tea she found the opportunity to ask some of the questions her mind teemed with. David told her that he and Mary had decided to part quite amicably in the end.

'We'd have destroyed each other,' he explained. 'I wasn't cut out to be a pampered invalid for the rest of my life, and I soon discovered that Mary found illness of any kind obscene.' He shook his head at her expression. 'Don't look like that, Robbie. She couldn't help it. We none of us can help the way we are. As it turns out it was the best thing that could have happened for me. At Meadowlands I learned that life really could begin again. I met this young guy, a brother of Sister Grey, who runs the place; a while ago he started a scheme for people like me. He converted a large house into specially adapted flats for us. We make handmade musical instruments and sell them. We're a co-operative and we're doing great business. We're hoping to expand soon. This evening I'm going to tell them all about it at Ennermoor. Maybe I'll get some new recruits.'

Robyn watched him as he spoke, his face alight with enthusiasm, and her heart lifted. Before his accident David had been an estate agent. He had liked his job, but she had never seen him as enthusiastic as this about it.

'You don't miss your old job, then?' she asked. 'You don't feel bitter about – about all that happened?'

He smiled his old heartwarming smile and reached out to ruffle her hair.

'Bitter? Good lord, no. Of course I have my off-days – days when I get impatient and feel sorry for myself, but we all have those, don't we? And they're getting fewer and fewer. There just isn't time for that kind of thing at Lyric House!'

Robyn stirred her tea thoughtfully. 'I always felt that you must blame me for what happened to you.'

He stared at her in stunned silence. *'Blame you?* Good God! Whatever gave you that idea?'

She shook her head. 'I think Mary blamed

me. And I know I certainly blamed myself. That's why I kept out of the way all this time – and when you didn't answer my letters...'

'Letters? I didn't get any letters!' David stopped and shook his head sadly. 'I can guess what happened, and I daresay you can too. I think the least said, the better, don't you?' He reached across the table to touch her hand. 'The main thing is I've found you again, eh? And now I want to hear all about you and this new career of yours. We've got some catching up to do!'

The staff at Ennermoor Hospital had put on quite a spread and the evening proved to be a great success. Mrs Rawlings came along, and was as impressed as her son was when she heard about David's struggle to conquer his disability and the Lyric House project. But another guest arrived halfway through the evening. She came late and stood at the back of the room, and it wasn't until David had finished speaking and they broke for supper that she made her presence known. David was the first to spot her and his face lit up.

'Well, by all that's wonderful! It's my favourite physio, old glamour-puss herself! Come and meet my baby sister.'

Robyn turned, and her eyes widened with surprise when she saw the object of David's overjoyed greeting was Fiona. She looked on as the other girl hugged her brother warmly.

'It's wonderful to see you again, David, and your sister and I know each other well.' Fiona smiled at Robyn. 'So you two *are* related, then?'

Robyn nodded. 'We'd lost touch. If it hadn't been for you I might never have found him again. It was quite a shock when you mentioned him that day at the cottage.'

Fiona smiled. 'I'm glad to have been the one to help you find him.' She turned to smile at David again. 'The trouble this guy used to give me, you wouldn't believe! But who can resist that smile?'

'Who indeed!'

David was leaning forward eagerly. 'Come on now, I want to hear all your news. What about that boy-friend of yours out in Saudi Arabia – the one who wanted to marry you? Have you finally seen sense and decided to throw him over in favour of me?'

Fiona laughed, her cheeks colouring a little. 'Same old David! It's a good job I'm not the shy, secretive kind.' She glanced at Robyn. 'Your sister already knows my news,

232

so I may as well tell you. I made up my mind at last. We're engaged.'

David gave a whoop of delight. 'Great! This calls for a celebration.' He pulled a face. 'Pity they don't allow any booze in here. We'll have to make do with coffee.' He raised his cup.

'Well, here's all the best to you both. To Fiona and...' He frowned. 'What's his name? I forget.'

'Martin,' Fiona supplied. 'Martin Fraser. He's a mechanical engineer, working for an oil company. He'll be back in this country soon, for Christmas, I hope, and we're hoping to be married early in the new year.'

'Fantastic!' said David. 'And then what – a life of domestic bliss – the patter of tiny feet?'

Fiona laughed. 'Who knows? Anything is possible. The only thing stopping me from marrying Martin all along was the career thing and my restless, itchy feet. But I have a very good doctor friend who talked to me like a Dutch uncle and made me see sense. Martin and I have come to a compromise.' She smiled happily. 'He's promised to stay in one place if I do too.'

David looked doubtful. 'Won't you find it boring, staying put?'

'No, you see we have new and exciting plans afoot in Crownhaven. It was supposed to be a secret, but the papers have got hold of it now, so I might as well tell you. We're starting a new health centre. My father's house is to be converted. It's much too large for him now that he's alone and I'm to be married.' She smiled at Robyn. 'We have a new dynamic young doctor to run it for us, haven't we, Robyn? And he's persuaded me to be resident physio, so there you are!'

The two continued to chatter, catching up on each other's news, but Robyn's thoughts were swirling dizzily in her head. It seemed she had things hopelessly muddled. It wasn't Ross Fiona was engaged to after all. And the new job she had spoken of – could that be the reason Ross and she had been together so much? That message on the answering machine – it was all so clear now that Fiona had been talking about that and about her decision to marry Martin. Ross must have taken her to Windermere that day to help her to sort out her problems.

Robyn's heart sank when she thought of the things she'd said to him. But why hadn't he denied any of them? One answer was blatantly clear: he simply hadn't thought it worth while. Fiona was still talking and she began to listen again.

'They've already started work on the house,' she was telling David. 'It's lucky I had my grandmother's flat to move into. It's on the ground floor of the block. I've been busy getting it ready for Martin and myself. Everything seems to be working out nicely for me at last.' She turned to look apologetically at Robyn. 'But I'm monopolising all your time together. I'm sorry, you must have so much to talk about.' She stood up. 'Do keep in touch, David. Maybe you and Robyn will come to my wedding. I'll send you an invitation.'

When she had gone Robyn was silent for a long moment until David reached out to touch her hand.

'What is it, Robbie?' he asked quietly. 'I was watching you. Something she said shook you, didn't it? Want to tell me about it?'

His soft voice and the hand that touched hers were almost more than she could bear, and tears filled her eyes as she looked at him.

'Oh, David,' she said brokenly, 'I've been such a fool – such a blind, stupid fool!'

CHAPTER TEN

For a long time they sat together in the little room Sister had prepared for David while he listened patiently to Robyn's outpourings. When she had finished he smiled sadly at her.

'Oh dear, you haven't changed much, have you, Robbie? Still a shade too proud for your own good – not to mention stubborn. I'd have thought this new job of yours would have ironed out some of those wrinkles.' He reached out to touch her hand. 'So what happens now?'

She shook her head. 'I don't know. All I *do* know is that I can't stay here.'

'But why?' he asked. 'Now that you know you had it all wrong. Don't tell me you don't know how to apologise gracefully! Haven't you learned your lesson, even now?'

She looked at him. 'It isn't quite that simple, David. You don't know Ross. He hasn't changed. I might have jumped to the wrong conclusions, but nothing has really altered. I honestly don't believe there's room for anything in his life but that driving ambition of his. He couldn't even be an ordinary GP – even that job had to be inflated to match his ego.'

David sighed. 'Why don't you go to him and have a talk; call some kind of truce while you sort things out? It seems to me that you've both got things a bit twisted.' He gave her a wry smile. 'If you ask me, I'd say you were too much in love to be seeing things straight!'

Robyn didn't answer, just bit her lip, unable to meet his eyes. He squeezed her hand. 'Look, it's Christmas in a couple of weeks. What are you doing? We're planning a great time at Lyric House, and you're welcome to join us. I'd love you to come and see my flat – meet the others. I can't wait to show you all off to each other.'

For a second her eyes lit up, then clouded as she remembered she would be on duty over the holiday.

'Oh, David, I'd have loved to come, but I've volunteered for duty. I thought I was going to be on my own, you see, and...' she broke off as her throat constricted. What a mess she'd made of everything! She'd looked forward to today so much, and now here she was trying not to cry in front of David.

'Hey, come on, cheer up,' he urged, peering into her face. 'There's always another time. Maybe you can come for New Year – that'll be just as much fun.'

She looked up at him. 'David, when I leave here, suppose I try and get a job somewhere in the Midlands? I'd be nearer you and...' She broke off as he shook his head.

'Listen, love,' he said gently, 'nothing would please me more than to have you near me. But as I said, you're not seeing things very clearly at the moment. You're in danger of taking that big leap, and I don't want to be a sort of safety net.'

She frowned. 'You think I'd be using you?'

'No, of course not,' he said firmly. 'I don't quite know how to put it without sounding brutal, but standing on your own two feet takes time and courage – I know that all too well. Sometimes, kind relatives just make it more difficult.'

She looked at him. 'Oh, David, you make me feel ashamed!'

As Robyn drove back to Ravenshore that night she had a lot to think about. It was odd, the way things worked out. If David hadn't come to Ennermoor this weekend she might never have discovered how wrong she'd been. She might have given in her notice and left, never knowing that Fiona was engaged to another man and not to Ross at all. Not that it made any difference. It was still too late. There had been too much wrangling between them for her ever to put things right now.

When she got back to the cottage she found it empty, and she remembered that Fay was out with Alan. She was grateful not to have to talk to anyone. She felt drained; her head aching with all that had happened. To have had to sit down and recount it all to someone, even Fay, would have been intolerable.

One thing brightened the following day for Robyn. When she and Jim got back to Control to sign off at the end of their shift she found a bouquet of flowers waiting for her. Attached was a card on which was written simply: *Thanks for what you did. Ron.*

Jim grinned at her. 'Hello, made a hit, have you?'

Robyn inhaled the fragrance of the yellow and bronze chrysanthemums happily. 'I don't know about that. It's nice to feel appreciated, though, isn't it?'

As she came out into the car park a voice hailed her and she looked round to see Bill waiting for her in his car. Seeing her, he got out and walked over, looking pointedly at the flowers in her arms.

'Well, what's this? I thought Harvest Festival was weeks ago!'

'Grateful patient,' she told him briefly. 'We're not supposed to accept presents, but this is more of a token.' She laughed. 'I don't think they quite knew what to do about it at Control. None of the fellows has ever had a bunch of flowers presented to them!' She looked at him. 'Where have you been, Bill? I haven't seen you for ages.'

He paused. 'Have you got time for a coffee?' He looked at his watch. 'Or a drink? It'll be opening time by the time we drive to the Feathers. We can go in my car.'

Robyn hesitated, 'Well, I did say I'd have dinner ready...' She stopped. Clearly Bill wanted to talk. There was an unusually sober look in his eyes as he turned to her. 'All right, wait while I put these flowers in the car and I'll be with you.'

The Feathers was two streets away from Control, and the bar was almost empty as they bought drinks and settled with them before the blazing log fire in the privacy of the snug. Robyn looked at him.

'What's wrong, Bill?'

'I'm leaving Crownhaven at Christmas,' he

241

told her. 'It was the piece I wrote about the new health centre. The editor approved it at the time, but some local bigwig took exception to it and kicked up a fuss.' He shrugged. 'Someone's head had to roll – guess whose?'

'Oh, Bill, I'm sorry. That seems so unfair.'

He took a long pull of his beer. 'All in the game, as they say.' He smiled at her. 'It may be a blessing in disguise. I haven't had much luck in this place. Anyway, I've found another job and the old man has given me a good reference, so it could be worse. I'm joining a paper down south the first week in the New Year. It sounds quite a lively place.' He grinned with a hint of the old bravado. 'You watch, I'll make one of the Nationals by the time I'm thirty yet!'

'Oh, Bill, I'm so glad for you!'

He looked at her for a long moment, his face suddenly serious. 'I was rather hoping you wouldn't be!' He gave her a wistful smile. 'It was never really on between us, was it? It's no accident that I haven't been in touch. I hoped you might miss me and ring, but you didn't.'

'I've been very busy, Bill.'

'I know.' He drank the last of his beer and looked at her. 'I've done a lot of thinking about us lately and, looking back, I realised when it started to look hopeless. I could almost tell you the exact day.' He shook his head. 'I must have been stupid not to have seen it before. It's St Clair, isn't it? You said you knew him before.' He shook his head impatiently. 'I can't think why it took me so long to put two and two together.'

Robyn was silent, lost for words. 'It's not on between Ross and me either, if it's any consolation,' she told him quietly.

He gave her a wry smile. 'It isn't. If he hadn't come along when he did I really think we might have worked it out, Robyn.' He waited for her to say something. When she didn't he stood up, picking up the glasses and looking at her enquiringly. 'Ah well, one for the road, then? It may be the last we have together.'

She looked up at him. 'All right, Bill. One for the road.'

That evening Robyn wrote out her notice. There was nothing here for her now – except memories of the new start she'd failed so miserably to make. She had no idea where she would go when she left Crownhaven. Maybe she could go and stay with David for a while until some new idea presented itself, though she didn't want him to think she was making a convenience of him.

She had missed Fay again this evening. The other girl was on night duty, but she had already eaten and gone out by the time Robyn arrived home, leaving a note to say that she was meeting Alan. Their relationship seemed to be growing quite serious lately and Robyn expected to hear news of an engagement any day now.

By nine-thirty she had made a fair copy of her resignation, signed it and sealed the envelope, putting it into her bag, ready to hand in in the morning. The task had depressed her. In spite of being the only woman on the unit she had formed a good working relationship with her male colleagues and been happy at Crownhaven.

She got up from the table and stretched. She would get ready for bed and then make a hot drink. An early night would do her good. She undressed, then came down to the kitchen in her dressing gown and measured milk into a pan; a cup of chocolate would help her to sleep. It was as she was taking the tin out of the cupboard that the front doorbell rang. She stopped, looking at her watch. Nine-forty-five. It was late for callers. Not many people came out to Ravenshore this late in the evening, especially at this time of year.

She turned off the gas under the milk pan and went through to the hall, tying the belt of her dressing gown securely round her waist. Through the glass panel she could see that the caller was tall and male. She opened the door a crack.

'Who is it?'

'Robyn – it's me, Ross.'

Her heart missed a beat. 'Oh!'

'Well, can I come in? It's freezing out here!'

'Oh – of course.' She held the door open for him. 'I – couldn't think who it could be at this time of the evening. I was just going to bed. Not many…' As she turned to face him he grasped her shoulders, making her catch her breath.

'Robyn, you stupid little idiot! You and I have some talking to do. And this time I'm not leaving here until we set things straight.'

There was barely room for them both in the tiny hallway and Robyn inclined her head towards the living-room. 'Shall we go in there?'

His hands dropped to his sides and he followed her into the room. They stood looking at each other for a moment, Robyn wondering what he could have heard to bring him here. Her mouth was dry as she said:

'I was just going to have a hot drink.

Would you like one?'

'Later.' Ross reached out and took her arm, pushing her down into a chair and sitting opposite her. 'After we've thrashed things out. I was up at the hospital earlier this evening, seeing a patient after surgery, and I ran into Fay. She congratulated me on my *engagement to Fiona!*'

Robyn blushed and looked away. 'Oh.'

'It seems that you and she had got the wrong idea.'

'I know. But I saw Fiona at the weekend and I realised I was wrong from what she said. I haven't seen Fay since. Fiona was telling my brother about her fiancé – she knows him, you see...'

'*Brother?*' He stared at her.

She nodded. 'David. I hadn't seen him for years – not since his accident. We lost touch. That's why I never mentioned him.' She looked up at him helplessly. 'There was a dreadful family row. He was the man who was paralysed in an accident – the reason why Danny Rawlings got to me so much.' She shook her head. 'Oh, it's all too complicated. You'd be bored to tears, hearing it all.' It was all so involved. How could she hope to make him understand? She began to turn away, but Ross caught her

246

arm, turning her towards him. The commanding tone of his voice made her look into his eyes.

'*Try* me, Robyn. Just try me. There's plenty of time. Neither of us is going anywhere. Take your time and tell me all about it – everything.'

She moistened her dry lips and began, slowly at first, then more rapidly, finding it an almost overwhelming relief to tell someone the whole story at last. When she had finished he looked at her for a long moment, his eyes incredulous.

'So all this time you've kept it locked away – all that needless guilt and unhappiness. And all for nothing. No wonder I felt I never really knew you!' He leaned towards her. 'When you walked out on me – before I went away – it all went back to this really, didn't it? This blow you took?'

Robyn looked at the hands clenched in her lap, the fingers tightly twined together. 'After what happened to David I suppose I lost a lot of my confidence. You restored it for me, Ross. You changed my life – and when you asked me to marry you I really believed it was because you couldn't leave without me – that you loved me that much.' She drew a deep breath and made herself look at him. 'Then I discovered that you needed a wife in order to get the job and everything changed. I felt so – so let down.'

Ross lifted her chin till her eyes were on a level with his. 'Oh, Robyn, why couldn't you have told me how you felt? Why couldn't you have tried to trust me?' His fingers were hard against her jawbone as he went on: 'Nothing in life is pure black and white – Fiona could tell you that. At least because of what you and I have been through I was able to help her make her mind up.' He laughed dryly. 'It's strange, the way it sometimes takes a complete outsider to make us see things clearly. That day Fiona and I spent together at Windermere we talked for hours. I made her see that she should marry the man she loves, and through talking to her a lot of things became clear to me too.' He shook his head. 'My ambition must have seemed hard and calculating to you, but it wasn't really. It didn't just happen either, you know. I wanted to get on because I saw the rut my father got himself into, stuck up there in a Highland village, miles from anywhere, going on year after year doling out the same treatments for the same ills. When I qualified I set my sights higher. I wanted to do more with my skills.'

'I know all that. I heard the message Fiona left for you on your answering machine. Knowing I got it all wrong just makes me feel a fool. But it's too late anyway. It's over. And – and I'm leaving here soon.'

There was a small silence, then he asked: 'You don't have to leave here because of me.'

Robyn spun round to face him, her eyes glistening with unshed tears. 'Well, why else would I leave?' she challenged. 'All right, so we've learned a little more about each other, but it doesn't change anything. You have an important new job lined up. I can work anywhere, so I'm obviously the one to move on. I'd already decided that.' She took the envelope containing her resignation from her bag and waved it at him. 'I'm handing this is in tomorrow.'

Ross stood up, looking down at her, his hands at his sides. 'I see. So that's your last word, is it? As uncompromising as ever! Don't you want to hear my view of it?'

'But I already know it. You've always wanted to be free,' she told him. 'You always intended your career to come first. I've seen nothing to persuade me that you've changed your mind.'

For answer he grasped her shoulders and drew her to him abruptly. His lips were hard as they took hers. It was more like a punishment than a measure of affection. She resisted, standing rigid and unyielding in the circle of his arms as he pressed her close. He released her at last, his eyes searching hers as his hands came up to cup her face.

'Does that tell you anything, Robyn?'

She stared up at him. His kiss had dashed the breath from her body and before she could recover enough to reply, his mouth was on hers again, this time gently and coaxingly, his lips moving sensuously against hers, parting her lips and exploring her mouth until she whimpered and melted against him, giving herself up to his growing passion. Her hands crept to his shoulders, then round his neck, caressing the strong, smooth column and burying her fingers in the softly curling hair at the back of his head. She felt his arms tighten around her, one hand moving down her spine, the fingers spreading to press her body close to his. She felt his need for her in every pulse-beat, and her response was involuntary.

At last he released her and they looked at each other. Robyn's whole being was in turmoil, all her defences stripped away in her aching love for him. There was a gleam of triumph in Ross's eyes as he sank on to the settee, pulling her down beside him.

'I knew you hadn't changed. Oh, Robbie – Robbie darling, how could you be such a stubborn little fool? Can't you see what I really want?'

His arms imprisoned her against him and her heart drummed wildly as she looked up at him. He laughed gently.

'Don't look at me like that! I want you to *marry* me, so for heaven's sake give me the answer before I shake it out of you!'

He kissed her again, taking her response for assent. When he released her she buried her face against his shoulder, too weak to speak. This time he meant it, surely? In any case she was past caring. She couldn't let him go again.

He loosened the belt of her dressing gown and bent to kiss the smooth skin of her shoulder, planting a line of tingling kisses all along the length of her collarbone until he reached the hollow of her throat. His hand was warm through the thin material of her nightdress and her pulses raced as the feather-light touch turned to urgent caresses. Slipping the narrow strap from her shoulder, he eased away the flimsy covering and cupped her breast, whispering her name softly as his lips lingered on hers.

It was some time before either of them spoke again, and when Ross glanced at his watch he saw with a shock that it was almost midnight.

'I suppose I should go,' he said reluctantly, his mouth against her hair. 'Tomorrow's a working day – unless…' he raised his head to look at her, and she reached up to brush his hair tenderly back from his forehead.

'Don't go, darling,' she whispered. 'There's so much I want to ask you – so much wasted time to make up.'

He sighed contentedly and relaxed again into the corner of the settee, pulling her back against him, his arms around her waist.

'Don't let's wait too long, Robbie. It'd be nice if we were married when the new health centre opens. There's to be a flat there for me – with a garden. A family home. It's a family doctor you're marrying, don't forget.'

Slowly, she disentangled herself from his arms and stood up, wrapping her dressing gown tightly round herself and tying the belt firmly. 'I think I'd like you to go now, Ross,' she said coolly.

He stared at her. 'What's the matter? Did I say something?'

'It's the same old story, isn't it?' she threw at him. 'The next thing on the agenda is a wife! A family doctor should be married ideally, shouldn't he? I'm just another qualification, like before. Why is it I never learn?'

His mouth dropped open in amazement. 'My God! You mean it, don't you? All right, so I need a wife. I also need you, Robbie. So what's wrong with the two going together?'

'I don't know that I want to marry you after all, Ross,' she told him stubbornly.

He threw up his hands in exasperation. 'I don't believe this!' he shouted. 'What do I have to do to convince you? Why do you find everything I do so suspect?'

Robyn turned away from him, catching her trembling lower lip between her teeth as the old suspicions took possession of her, picking her up and carrying her along with gathering impetus. When he met Fiona in Saudi Arabia and heard about her father's practice he made a bid for her affections. But when he realised she was in love with someone else, he didn't give up – oh no! It was too good a chance to pass up. He could still come to Crownhaven and take over the practice – work it up into a flourishing health centre. How convenient it must have been to find her here, a ready-made wife, just waiting to fall into his arms! Another thought struck her and she rounded on him.

'You even got rid of the opposition, didn't you? It was *you* who got Bill sacked from the *Courier?*'

He stared at her. 'Why on earth would I do that?'

'Because he was in the way. In more ways than one,' she told him furiously. 'He was stirring up public reaction to the new centre *and* threatening to take your – your *instant fiancée!*'

Ross sprang to his feet, his eyes flashing with anger. 'I think you've said enough. Stop it, Robyn! Stop it before you go too far.'

'Before *I* go too far?' She was too wound up to stop now. 'I said before that you trample on people to get what you want, and it's true. I *hate* you, Ross!'

The slap she delivered to his face rang out as sharply as a pistol shot and the sound brought her abruptly to her senses. She stared at him numbly, holding her breath, her temper deflating like a pricked balloon. It was as though time stood still. As she watched the marks of her fingers etch themselves across his cheek like a brand she felt her whole body begin to tremble. Catching her lower lip between her teeth, she took a faltering step towards him, reaching out her hand.

254

'Oh!– Oh, Ross, I…'

But he turned abruptly away. At the door he paused, turning to look at her. 'It's as well I found out what you think of me now, before it's too late,' he said coldly. 'I should have left well alone. You were right in one thing, Robyn – no place on earth is big enough to hold both of us.'

She stood in the empty room long after the sound of his car had retreated into the quiet night. Her mind was numb as she registered the familiar sounds: the fire crackling, the distant roar of the sea, the ticking of the clock. She shivered and realised that she was cold. In the hall she closed the door that Ross had left open. It was only as she returned to the empty room that the full significance of all that had been said hit her. It was really over this time. She had driven him away with her accusations. But, true or not, there was still one indisputable fact. *What do I have to do to convince you?* Ross had said, missing the most basic point of all. The one short sentence he had never uttered and that she longed to hear him say: *Robyn darling, I love you.*

Somehow she got through the days that followed, throwing herself wholeheartedly into her work. Her resignation was accepted with regret and a small party was given for her. It was hard to keep the tears at bay, hearing her colleagues praise her, telling her how much her work had been appreciated. They had even collected enough money to buy her a handsome present, a smart vanity case a top model would have been proud of. It was a very traumatic time and she wished heartily that it could be over as soon as possible.

On her last day off she went to Ennermoor to say goodbye to Danny Rawlings and heard the good news that he had applied for a trainee place at Lyric House. He was to be interviewed, but David had already recommended him, so he stood a good chance. On the way home Robyn asked Mrs Rawlings what she thought of the prospect. The older woman sighed resignedly.

'I've come to terms with the fact that he must make his own life,' she said. 'After all, he won't always have me around to look after him, will he?' She smiled. 'In the meantime, he knows I'm here if he needs me. And if he asks…' She looked at Robyn. 'I said *if*, mind; – I could always move down there to be a little nearer.'

Robyn smiled her approval. It was good that she had at least done some good during her time here.

Christmas moved inexorably nearer and everyone was in a fever of preparation. At Control the decorations went up; brightly coloured paper chains festooned the rest room and the canteen. The talk was all of parties, children and visiting mothers-in-law. Jim was to play Santa at the local children's home and at Fell Cottage there was a small celebration as Fay and Alan announced their engagement. Robyn tried hard to be part of it all, but her heart wasn't in it. All she really wanted was for Christmas to be over so that she could leave. She shopped for a present for David and one for Fay. She bought an engagement present too and presented it to the happy couple, stifling her own unhappiness as she watched their delight in each other.

She was glad to have plenty of hard work to occupy her. The weather had worsened again, the snow bringing with it the usual crop of ills and accidents. Christmas week was busy with the predictable minor incidents, mainly caused through too much celebrating.

Fay went home for the holiday on the day before Christmas Eve, and her going left the cottage feeling cold and empty. Somehow,

257

to Robyn, it wasn't home any more, and she was quite glad to leave it and report for duty the following day.

The atmosphere at Control was festive. There was turkey on the menu in the canteen and a tape of carols being played to complete the Christmas atmosphere. Ruby Two went out to several minor calls. The shift went smoothly and uneventfully until the 999 call came through at sixteen hundred hours.

There had been an accident at one of the level crossings on the edge of the town. Severe frost had prevented the continental-type arm from lowering and a train had ploughed into a car that had been crossing. The engine and first carriage were derailed and there were several casualties.

With the exception of the non-emergency vehicle, all ambulances as well as the fire brigade and the local Integrated Voluntary Emergency Service were called to the incident, and Ruby Two was the second vehicle to arrive on the scene.

Robyn and Jim surveyed the chaos. The engine and the first coach had jack-knifed and the engine was tilted drunkenly. Under it lay the twisted wreckage of the car, and firemen were helping a team already on the scene to remove the only occupant, a middle-aged man with severe injuries. As Jim ran across to them he asked:

'Anyone else in there?'

One of the firemen answered: 'No, but I think there's someone else under the engine. We'll have to clear some of this wreckage away before we can get to her, though.'

Less severely injured victims were beginning to climb down from the train and police moved in to help them to safety and to control the crowd of onlookers that had gathered.

Jim collected their protective headgear and satchels from the ambulance and they went to work, attending to minor injuries as the victims were freed. They were on their way back to the ambulance when one of the firemen called to them:

'Could the lady come over here, please?'

Robyn crossed to the derailed engine and the man looked at her. 'We've got most of the wreckage clear now. I reckon you could just about squeeze in,' he told her. 'The victim seems to be conscious. She's writhing about a bit – might damage herself further.'

Without waiting to hear more, Robyn dropped on all fours and began to crawl under the engine. The light was poor and she called to Jim:

'Can you get me a lamp?' She heard his assent and edged forward, speaking softly to the victim:

'It's all right, help's on its way. Can you hear me?'

A tortured groan was the only reply.

Robyn edged further in, feeling the sharp stones cutting into her knees and hands. She knew that Jim would bring all the necessary gear, including the pain-relieving gas and oxygen.

With the help of the lamp that he passed to her she found that the victim was a young woman of about her own age. She was twisting and writhing in agony, and Robyn could see at once that her right leg was broken. There was a nasty gash above her eye and the other lacerations, as well as bleeding from the nose and ears. She edged alongside her and hooked the lamp to a piece of projecting metal, then steadied the girl's head, using her pencil torch to check her level of consciousness by the size of her pupils. The girl tried to say something, but Robyn couldn't make out the jumble of words.

'Don't try to talk,' she said gently. 'We'll have you out of here in no time.'

Jim bent down and peered in at her. 'How

is she?'

Robyn felt for the girl's pulse. It was thin and thready. 'Not too good,' she whispered. 'She's severely shocked and I suspect a skull fracture.'

'A medical team has just arrived,' Jim told her. 'The doctor's here now.'

Robyn heaved a sigh of relief. She didn't like the look of the girl and knew that there was no time to be lost if she were to be saved. She returned her attention to the patient until a voice addressed her:

'You'd better come out of there now. The lifting gear is ready. They're going to try to raise the engine so that we can get her out.'

She directed the beam of the lamp at Ross's face.

'I'm staying,' she told him briefly.

'Don't be a fool. Come out,' he commanded. Robyn shook her head.

'I can't leave her. I'll be all right.'

'What are her injuries?' he asked.

She told him, and he withdrew without further argument.

The next few minutes were like a nightmare. As she waited for the huge engine that hung above them to be lifted she applied what help she could to the injured girl, then lay close to her, holding her breath while the

261

heavy metal chassis above them creaked and groaned. Inch by inch it was raised until the gap widened and more light filtered in. Suddenly she saw Ross crouching close to where they lay.

'Right, come out now and let me in.' He reached in to grasp her arm.

She didn't argue, wriggling eel-like over the rails to allow him to take her place. Jim reached out to take her arm, helping her to her feet.

'Atta girl!' He had a trolley-bed ready. 'Most of the other victims have been taken to hospital now, thank God. There are no fatalities so far, though I didn't like the look of the car driver...'

'Look out, she's going!'

At the shout they both sprang back, and Robyn gave an involuntary cry as there was a sudden scream of metal. The engine, held by the lifting gear, seemed to sink back again before their horrified eyes. They heard the sickening screech of tearing metal, followed by a deafening bang – then silence as a doom-like cloud of dust engulfed them.

CHAPTER ELEVEN

'I really think you should go home now and get some rest.'

A gentle hand roused Robyn from the doze she had slipped into, and she opened her eyes to see a calm face peering into hers. She shook her head, finding her neck painfully stiff and her mouth dry. The hand on her shoulder tightened.

'Here, I've brought you a cup of tea. Drink it up.'

Robyn took it, sipping the hot liquid gratefully.

Looking round, she found the waiting room empty. When she had first arrived here it had been full of anxious relatives, waiting to see victims of the train crash. She glanced up at the clock on the wall and was shocked to see that it was after eleven. The Sister smiled, following her gaze.

'Yes, you've been here almost five hours.'

'Is there any change?' Robyn asked. 'Has he come round yet?'

The Sister shook her head. 'Not yet, but

he isn't in any danger, you know. It's just severe concussion. Every care is being taken. He'll be fine after a good rest, I promise you.'

'I know. I just want to be there when he wakes,' Robyn said. 'If I could just go in, I'll sit very quietly, I promise.'

Sister looked at her ruefully. 'Sure you wouldn't like to go home and freshen up?'

For the first time Robyn looked down at herself and realised what a sight she was. Her uniform was still caked with oil and dirt from the railway track and she guessed that her face and hair were grimy too. She nodded.

'I'll go along to the washroom. I'm sorry about this.'

Sister straightened her back and sighed resignedly. 'Oh well, off you go then, if you're determined to stay. When you come back you can sit with him awhile, but I warn you, he may not wake for some time yet.'

Ross was in a small side ward on his own and Sister had placed the most comfortable chair she could find at the bedside.

'I understand you're on duty again tomorrow,' she whispered. 'You're not going to be much use if you don't get some sleep.'

Robyn smiled wearily. 'I'll be fine as long

264

as he is,' she insisted. 'I have to be here when he wakes. I have something very important to tell him, you see.'

The Sister paused in the doorway. 'Well, I'll leave you. You know where I am if you want anything.'

Robyn pulled the chair up close to the bed and settled down to wait. The relief that Ross was going to be all right was almost overwhelming. The past few hours had been like the worst kind of nightmare. Leaning forward, she studied his face anxiously. There was a dark bruise along his right cheekbone and the gash at the hairline that had looked so gory and frightening when they first got him out had been neatly stitched. She reached out to stroke the bright hair and thought she saw his eyelids flutter slightly. Withdrawing her hand, she sank back wearily in the chair. Every muscle and bone in her body ached. She longed to sleep, but she didn't dare. When Ross wakened she wanted hers to be the first face he saw. Even if he turned away from her she had to be here; had to say what must be said.

Leaning back in the chair, she reflected yet again on her feelings when they had dragged him out from under the wrecked engine. It had seemed to take an age for the lifting gear to be re-engaged, and she had gone through agonies wondering what they would find. She knew she could never have forgiven herself for the things she had said to Ross if anything unthinkable had happened to him.

They had reached the girl first and rushed her off to hospital in one of the vehicles that had returned. Then Ross had been brought out by Jim, helped by one of the firemen. They had refused to let her go under the wreckage again, even though she had pleaded with them to let her.

Restless, she got up and went to the window. She couldn't erase the nightmare image imprinted on her mind; his limp body and lifeless face when at last they got him out. The blood that had made her fear the worst; reminding her of the night David had been injured. If Ross should come out of it like that! Broken – paralysed! She closed her eyes tightly as though trying to shut out the memory.

Drawing back the curtains, she looked out across the snow-covered car park. On the far side she could see the floodlit spire of St Mary's church, and as she stood there the bells began to peal for the midnight service.

Suddenly she remembered. It was almost Christmas.

Behind her a small sound made her turn. At last Ross was stirring. Her heart leaping, she moved closer. His eyelids fluttered and opened. For a moment the grey-blue eyes looked uncomprehendingly into hers, then he smiled.

'Robbie.' He looked around him. 'What am I doing here? What happened?'

Robyn took his hand. 'It's all right. You were treating a victim of the train crash, remember? The lifting gear slipped and you were trapped underneath the engine.'

'That's right.' An anxious expression crossed his face as he took in her dishevelled appearance. 'My God! I remember now – are *you* all right?'

'I'm fine,' she assured him. 'And so is the patient. You saved her life.'

He frowned. 'You wouldn't come out from under that damned wreckage – never would do as you were told. Stubborn little idiot!' His hand gripped hers tightly.

'Ross...' She bent closer. 'I've been here ever since we brought you in. I wanted to be here when you woke. There's something I have to say. I – I'm sorry.'

'Sorry? What for?'

'For the things I said – for losing my temper – for slapping you.' She touched the bruise on his cheek tenderly, feeling almost that she had caused it. 'Can you forgive me?'

Ross frowned. 'I haven't the slightest idea what you're talking about.'

Robyn looked at him in surprise. 'But – the other night – at the cottage...'

'Ever heard of amnesia?' he asked, the ghost of a twinkle in his eyes. 'A bang on the head sometimes does funny things.' He reached out to stroke her hair, drawing her head down towards him. 'I can remember *some* of the things that happened that night, though. I remember asking you to marry me, for instance, and I seem to remember that you didn't say no.'

'Oh, Ross!' she smiled.

'There's another thing I don't remember,' he went on. 'I can't think why, but I don't remember ever telling you I love you.' His eyes looked into hers. 'I do, Robbie, and if you love me too there can't be much else that matters, can there?'

She bent to kiss him. 'Nothing, darling. Nothing in the world,' she whispered. 'I'll have to go now, but I'll be back tomorrow – and all the other tomorrows. I'm never going to let you go again, not after tonight. I thought I'd lost you, you see; lost you for...' She looked up to find that he had drifted off to sleep again, a smile on his lips. Very gently, she kissed him and tiptoed out of the room.

The cold night air turned her breath to plumes as she walked across the car park. Newly fallen snow squeaked under her feet. Her mind knew she was tired and must get what sleep she could before daylight, but her heart was on another plane, soaring far above the daily routine.

The sound of the church bells filled her ears, crystal clear on the frosty air, filling her heart with grateful joy as she climbed into her car. Soon they would ring for her and Ross. This time nothing would stop them!

The publishers hope that this book has given you enjoyable reading. Large Print Books are especially designed to be as easy to see and hold as possible. If you wish a complete list of our books please ask at your local library or write directly to:

Dales Large Print Books
Magna House, Long Preston,
Skipton, North Yorkshire.
BD23 4ND